PINAFORE PALACE

PINAFORE PALACE

A BOOK OF RHYMES FOR THE NURSERY

EDITED BY

Kate Douglas (Smith) Wiggin, 1856-1923, ed.

and

Nora Archibald Smith, 1859-1934, joint ed.

Granger Index Reprint Series

BOOKS FOR LIBRARIES PRESS
PLAINVIEW, NEW YORK

PN
6110
.C4
W458
1972

Wiggin, Kate Douglas (Smith) 1856-1923, ed.
    Pinafore Palace; a book of rhymes for the nursery,
edited by Kate Douglas Wiggin and Nora Archibald Smith.
    (Granger index reprint series)
    SUMMARY: A collection of pems poems and nursery rhymes
for the very young.
    Original ed. issued in series: McClure's library
of chidren's classics.
    1. Nursery rhymes. 2. Children's poetry.
    [1. Nursery rymes. 2. Poetry-Collections]
    I. Smith, Nora Archibald, 1859-1934, joint ed.
    II. Title. III. Series: McClure's library of
children's classics.
    PN6110.C4W458 1972   398.8   72-8290
    ISBN 0-8369-6399-7

PREFACE

TO THE MOTHER

" A Court as of angels,
A public not to be bribed,
Not to be entreated,
Not to be overawed."

Such is the audience—in long clothes or short frocks, in pinafores or kilts, or in the brief trousers that bespeak the budding man—such is the crowing, laughing court, the toddling public that awaits these verses.

Every home, large or small, poor or rich, that has a child in it, is a Pinafore Palace, and we have borrowed the phrase from one of childhood's most whimsical and devoted poets-laureate, thinking no other words would so well express our meaning.

If the two main divisions of the book—" The Royal Baby " and " Little Prince and Princess "—should seem to you a trifle sentimental it will be because you forget for the moment the gayety

▼

and humor of the title with its delightful assumptions of regal dignity and state. Granted the Palace itself, everything else falls easily into line, and if you cannot readily concede the royal birth and bearing of your neighbor's child you will see nothing strange in thinking of your own nursling as little prince or princess, and so you will be able to accept gracefully the sobriquet of Queen Mother, which is yours by the same invincible logic!

Oh, yes, we allow that instead of being gravely editorial in our attitude, we have played with the title, as well as with all the sub-titles and classifications, feeling that it was the next pleasantest thing to playing with the babies themselves. It was so delightful to re-read the well-loved rhymes of our own childhood and try to find others worthy to put beside them; so delicious to imagine the hundreds of young mothers who would meet their old favorites in these particular pages; and so inspiring to think of the thousands of new babies whose first hearing of nursery classics would be associated with this red-covered volume, that we found ourselves in a joyous mood which we hope will be contagious. Nothing is surer than that a certain gayety of heart and mind constitute the most whole-

some climate for young children. "The baby whose mother has not charmed him in his cradle with rhyme and song has no enchanting dreams; he is not gay and he will never be a great musician," so runs the old Swiss saying.

Youthful mothers, beautifully and properly serious about their strange new duties and responsibilities, need not fear that Mother Goose is anything but healthful nonsense. She holds a place all her own, and the years that have rolled over her head (some of the rhymes going back to the sixteenth century) only give her a firmer footing among the immortals. There are no real substitutes for her unique rhymes, neither can they be added to nor imitated; for the world nowadays is seemingly too sophisticated to frame just this sort of merry, light-hearted, irresponsible verse which has mellowed with the years. "These ancient rhymes," says Andrew Lang, "are smooth stones from the brook of time, worn round by constant friction of tongues long silent."

Nor is your use of this "light literature of the infant scholar" in the nursery without purpose or value. You are developing ear, mind, and heart, and laying a foundation for a later love of the best things in poetry. Whatever else we may do or leave undone, if we wish to widen the spiritual horizon of our children let us not close the windows on the emotional and imaginative sides. " There is in every one of us a poet whom the man has outlived." Do not let the poetic instinct die of inanition; keep it alive in the child by feeding his youthful ardor, strengthening his insight, guarding the sensitiveness and delicacy of his early impressions, and cherishing the fancies that are indeed " the trailing clouds of glory" he brings with him " from God who is his home."

The rhythm of verse will charm his senses even in his baby days; later on he will feel the beauty of some exquisite lyric phrase as keenly as you do, for the ear will have been opened and will be satisfied only with what is finest and best.

The second division of the book " Little Prince and Princess" will take the children out of the nursery into the garden, the farmyard, and the world outside the Palace, where they will meet and play with their fellows in an ever-widening circle of social activity. " Baby's Hush-a-byes" in cradle or mother's lap will now give place to the quiet cribside talks called " The Palace Bed Time" and " The Queen Mother's Counsel"; and in the story hour " The Palace Jest-Book" *will furnish merriment for the youngsters who laughed the year before over the simpler nonsense of Mother Goose.*

When the pinafores themselves are cast aside Pinafore Palace will be outgrown, and you can find something better suited to the developing requirements of the nursery folk in " The Posy Ring." Then the third volume in our series— " Golden Numbers "—will give boys and girls from ten to fifteen a taste of all the best and soundest poetry suitable to their age, and after that they may enter on their full birthright, "the rich deposit of the centuries."

No greater love for a task nor happiness in doing it, no more ardent wish to please a child or meet a mother's need, ever went into a book than have been wrought into this volume and its three predecessors. We hope that it will find its way into the nurseries where wealth has provided every means of ministering to the young child's growth in body, mind, and soul; and if some of the Pinafore Palaces should be neat little kitchens, what joy it would be to think of certain young queen-mothers taking a breath between tasks to sit by the fire and read to their royal babies while the bread is baking, the kettle boiling, or the potatoes bubbling in the pot.

PREFACE

" Where does Pinafore Palace stand?
Right in the middle of Lilliput Land."

*And Lilliput Land is (or ought to be) the free-
est country in the universe. Its shining gates
open wide at dawn, closing only at sunset, and
toddling pilgrims with eager faces enter and
wander about at will. Decked in velvet or clad
in rags the friendly porter pays no heed, for the
pinafores hide all class distinctions.*

" We're bound for Pinafore Palace, sir,"
They say to the smiling gatekeeper.
" Do we need, if you please, an entrance ticket
Before we pass through your magic wicket? "
" Oh, no, little Prince and Princess dear,
All pinafores freely enter here! "

KATE DOUGLAS WIGGIN.

A CKNOWLEDGMENTS *are herewith made to the following pub-lishers for permission to include in this volume selections from their copyrighted publications:*

Houghton, Mifflin & Co.: "A Dewdrop" and "Bees," from Little Folk Lyrics, by Frank Dempster Sherman; "The Brown Thrush," from Childhood Songs, by Lucy Larcom; "Bossy and Daisy," from The Old Garden, by Margaret Deland; "Lost," from Poems for Children, by Celia Thaxter; "Clothes," "A Music Box," and "Learn-ing to Play," from A Pocketful of Posies, by Abbie Farwell Brown.

Lothrop, Lee & Shepard: "How they Sleep" and "The Darling Birds," from Babyland; "Follow Me," "Annie's Garden," "Good Mooly Cow," "The New Moon," "Do You Guess it is I," and "Baby's Birthday," from Little Songs, by Eliza Lee Follen; "Who Likes the Rain" and "Spring Questions," by Clara Doty Bates; and five poems by Emilie Poulsson as follows: "Chickens in Trouble" (Trans-lated from the Norwegian) and "A Puppy's Problem," from Through the Farmyard Gate; "The Story of Baby's Blanket," "The Story of Baby's Pillow," and "Baby's Breakfast," from Child Stories and Rhymes.

Little, Brown & Company: "The Owl, the Eel and the Warming Pan" and "The Difference," from Sundown Songs, by Laura E. Richards.

Milton Bradley Company: "The Five Little Fairies," "The Pigeons," "The Barnyard," from Rhymes for Little Hands, by Maud Burn-ham.

New England Publishing Company: "Our Mother," from the American Primary Teacher.

Small, Maynard & Company: "Hospitality," "The Child's Star," "Foot Soldiers," from Child Verse, by John B. Tabb.

The Outlook: "Baby's Journey," by Mary F. Butts.

And our thanks and tribute to the shade of "Mother Goose," beloved nurse of all who lisp the English tongue.

CONTENTS

PART I

THE ROYAL BABY

PART II

LITTLE PRINCE AND PRINCESS

PUBLIC NOTICE.—*This is to state,*
That these are the specimens left at the gate
Of Pinafore Palace, exact to date,
In the hands of the porter, Curlypate,
Who sits in his plush on a chair of state,
By somebody who is a candidate
For the Office of Lilliput Laureate.

William Brighty Rands.

PART I

THE ROYAL BABY

I

BABY'S PLAYS

I

Brow bender,
Eye peeper,
Nose smeller,
Mouth eater,
Chin chopper.
Knock at the door—peep in,
Lift up the latch—walk in.

Eye winker,
Tom Tinker,
Nose smeller,
Mouth eater,
Chin chopper.
Chin chopper.

Here sits the Lord Mayor,
Here sit his two men,
Here sits the cock,
And here sits the hen;
Here sit the chickens,
And here they go in,
Chippety, chippety, chippety chin.

3

Ring the bell!
Knock at the door!
Lift up the latch!
Walk in!

Pat-a-cake, pat-a-cake, baker's man!
So I do, master, as fast as I can:
Pat it, and prick it, and mark it with T,
Put it in the oven for Tommy and me.

Pease porridge hot,
    Pease porridge cold,
Pease porridge in the pot,
    Nine days old.
Some like it hot,
    Some like it cold,
Some like it in the pot,
    Nine days old.

Pat it, kiss it,
Stroke it, bless it;
Three days' sunshine, three days' rain,
Little hand all well again.

Warm, hands, warm, daddy's gone to plough;
If you want to warm hands, warm hands now.

Clap, clap handies,
Mammie's wee, wee ain;
Clap, clap handies,
Daddie's comin' hame;
Hame till his bonny wee bit laddie;
Clap, clap handies,
My wee, wee ain.

This little pig went to market;
This little pig stayed at home;
This little pig had roast beef;
This little pig had none;
This little pig said, " Wee, wee!
I can't find my way home."

Shoe the horse, and shoe the mare;
But let the little colt go bare.

Foot Soldiers

'Tis all the way to Toe-town,
  Beyond the Knee-high hill,
That Baby has to travel down
  To see the soldiers drill.

One, two, three, four, five, a-row—
A captain and his men—
And on the other side, you know,
Are six, seven, eight, nine, ten.

John B. Tabb.

How many days has my baby to play?
Saturday, Sunday, Monday,
Tuesday, Wednesday, Thursday, Friday,
Saturday, Sunday, Monday.

Dance to your daddy,
My little babby;
Dance to your daddy,
My little lamb.

You shall have a fishy,
In a little dishy;
You shall have a fishy
When the boat comes in.

One, Two

One, two,
Buckle my shoe;

Three, four,
Knock at the door;

Five, six,
Pick up sticks;

Seven, eight,
Lay them straight;

Nine, ten,
A good fat hen;

Eleven, twelve,
Let them delve;

Thirteen, fourteen,
Maids a-courting;

Fifteen, sixteen,
Maids in the kitchen;

Seventeen, eighteen,
Maids a-waiting;

Nineteen, twenty,
My plate's empty.

Merry are the bells, and merry would they ring;
Merry was myself, and merry could I sing;
With a merry ding-dong, happy, gay, and free,
And a merry sing-song, happy let us be!

Merry have we met, and merry have we been;
Merry let us part, and merry meet again;
With our merry sing-song, happy, gay, and free,
And a merry ding-dong, happy let us be!

Bow-wow-wow!
Whose dog art thou?
Little Tom Tinker's dog,
Bow-wow-wow!

Blow, wind, blow! and go, mill, go!
That the miller may grind his corn;
That the baker may take it,
And into rolls make it,
And send us some hot in the morn.

The Difference

Eight fingers,
    Ten toes,
Two eyes,
    And one nose.
Baby said
    When she smelt the rose,
"Oh! what a pity
    I've only one nose!"

Ten teeth
  In even rows,
Three dimples,
  And one nose.
Baby said
  When she smelt the snuff,
"Deary me!
  One nose is enough."

                 Laura E. Richards.

The Five Little Fairies
Finger-Play

Said this little fairy,
"I'm as thirsty as can be!"

Said this little fairy,
"I'm hungry, too! dear me!"

Said this little fairy,
"Who'll tell us where to go?"

Said this little fairy,
"I'm sure that I don't know!"

Said this little fairy,
"Let's brew some Dew-drop Tea!"
So they sipped it and ate honey
    Beneath the maple tree.

                 Maud Burnham.

The Pigeons

Ten snowy white pigeons are standing in line,
On the roof of the barn in the warm sunshine.

Ten snowy white pigeons fly down to the
    ground,
To eat of the grain that is thrown all around.

Ten snowy white pigeons soon flutter aloof,
And sit in a line on the ridge of the roof.

Ten pigeons are saying politely, " Thank you! "
If you listen, you hear their gentle " Coo-roo! "
                     Maud Burnham.

The Barnyard

When the Farmer's day is done,
In the barnyard, ev'ry one,
Beast and bird politely say,
" Thank you for my food to-day."

The cow says, " Moo! "
The pigeon, " Coo! "
The sheep says, " Baa! "
The lamb says, " Maa! "
The hen, " Cluck! Cluck! "
" Quack! " says the duck;

The dog, " Bow Wow! "
The cat, " Meow! "
The horse says, " Neigh!
I love sweet hay! "
The pig near by,
Grunts in his sty.

When the barn is locked up tight,
Then the Farmer says, " Good-night! "
Thanks his animals, ev'ry one,
For the work that has been done.

Maud Burnham.

PART I

THE ROYAL BABY

II

BABY'S HUSH-A-BYES

II

BABY'S HUSH-A-BYES

Hush-a-bye, baby, on the tree-top,
When the wind blows the cradle will rock;
When the bough breaks the cradle will fall,
Down will come baby, bough, cradle, and all.

Rock-a-bye, baby, thy cradle is green;
Father's a nobleman, mother's a Queen;
Betty's a lady, and wears a gold ring;
And Johnny's a drummer, and drums for the
    King.

Bye, baby bunting,
Daddy's gone a-hunting,
To get a little rabbit-skin,
To wrap his baby bunting in.

Hush thee, my babby,
Lie still with thy daddy,

Thy mammy has gone to the mill,
To grind thee some wheat
To make thee some meat,
And so, my dear babby, lie still.

Sleep, baby, sleep!
Thy father watches the sheep;
Thy mother is shaking the dream-land tree,
And down falls a little dream on thee:
Sleep, baby, sleep!

Sleep, baby, sleep!
The large stars are the sheep,
The wee stars are the lambs, I guess,
The fair moon is the shepherdess:
Sleep, baby, sleep!

From the German.

When little Birdie bye-bye goes,
Quiet as mice in churches,
He puts his head where no-one knows,
On one leg he perches.

When little Babie bye-bye goes,
On Mother's arm reposing,
Soon he lies beneath the clothes,
Safe in the cradle dozing.

When pretty Pussy goes to sleep,
Tail and nose together,
Then little mice around her creep,
Lightly as a feather.

When little Babie goes to sleep,
And he is very near us,
Then on tip-toe softly creep,
That Babie may not hear us.
Lullaby! Lullaby! Lulla, Lulla, Lullaby!
Unknown.

PART I

THE ROYAL BABY

III

BABY'S JOURNEYS

III

BABY'S JOURNEYS

Ride a cock-horse to Banbury Cross,
To see an old lady upon a white horse,
Rings on her fingers, and bells on her toes,
She shall have music wherever she goes.

This is the way the ladies ride;
    Tri, tre, tre, tree,
    Tri, tre, tre, tree!
This is the way the ladies ride,
    Tri, tre, tre, tre, tri-tre-tre-tree!

This is the way the gentlemen ride;
    Gallop-a-trot,
    Gallop-a-trot!
This is the way the gentlemen ride,
    Gallop-a-gallop-a-trot!

This is the way the farmers ride;
    Hobbledy-hoy,
    Hobbledy-hoy!
This is the way the farmers ride,
    Hobbledy, hobbledy-hoy!

Ride, baby, ride,
Pretty baby shall ride,
And have a little puppy-dog tied to her side,
And a little pussy-cat tied to the other,
And away she shall ride
To see her grandmother,
To see her grandmother,
To see her grandmother in London town.

See-saw sacradown,
Which is the way to London town?
One foot up, the other foot down,
That is the way to London town.

To market, to market,
To buy a plum bun;
Home again, home again,
Market is done.

Dance, little baby, dance up high,
Never mind, baby, mother is by;
Crow and caper, caper and crow,
There, little baby, there you go;

Up to the ceiling, down to the ground,
Backwards and forwards, round and round;
Dance, little baby, and mother will sing,
With the merry chorus, ding, ding, ding!

A farmer went trotting
  Upon his gray mare;
Bumpety, bumpety, bump!
With his daughter behind him,
  So rosy and fair;
Lumpety, lumpety, lump!

A raven cried "Croak";
  And they all tumbled down;
Bumpety, bumpety, bump!
The mare broke her knees,
  And the farmer his crown;
Lumpety, lumpety, lump.

The mischievous raven
  Flew laughing away;
Bumpety, bumpety, bump!
And vowed he would serve them
  The same the next day;
Bumpety, bumpety, bump!

Hey, my kitten, my kitten,
  And hey, my kitten, my deary!
Such a sweet pet as this
  Was neither far nor neary.

Here we go up, up, up,
  And here we go down, down, downy;
And here we go backwards and forwards,
  And here we go round, round, roundy.

Hey diddle, dinkety, poppety, pet,
The merchants of London they wear scarlet;
Silk in the collar and gold in the hem,
So merrily march the merchantmen.

Rhymes About a Little Woman

This is the way the ladies ride—
Saddle-a-side, saddle-a-side!

This is the way the gentlemen ride—
Sitting astride, sitting astride!

This is the way the grandmothers ride—
Bundled and tied, bundled and tied!

This is the way the babykins ride—
Snuggled inside, snuggled inside!

This is the way when they are late,
They *all* fly over a five-barred gate.

William Canton.

Every evening Baby goes
   Trot, trot, to town—
Across the river, through the fields,
   Up hill and down.

Trot, trot, the Baby goes,
   Up hill and down,
To buy a feather for her hat,
   To buy a woolen gown.

Trot, trot, the Baby goes;
   The birds fly down, alack!
" You cannot have our feathers, dear,"
   They say; " so please trot back."

Trot, trot, the Baby goes;
   The lambs come bleating near.
" You cannot have our wool," they say;
   " But we are sorry, dear."

Trot, trot, the Baby goes,
   Trot, trot, to town.
She buys a red rose for her hat,
   She buys a cotton gown.

Mary F. Butts.

PART I

THE ROYAL BABY

IV

BABY'S FRIENDS

IV

BABY'S FRIENDS

Mary had a pretty bird,
    Feathers bright and yellow,
Slender legs; upon my word,
    He was a pretty fellow.

The sweetest notes he always sang,
    Which much delighted Mary;
And near the cage she'd often sit,
    To hear her own Canary.

Lady-bird, lady-bird, fly away home,
Thy house is on fire, thy children all gone:
All but one whose name is Ann,
And she crept under the pudding-pan.

There was a little nobby colt,
    His name was Nobby Gray;
His head was made of pouce straw,
    His tail was made of hay.
        He could ramble, he could trot,
        He could carry a mustard-pot
        Round the town of Woodstock,
        Hey, Jenny, hey!

The north wind doth blow,
And we shall have snow,
And what will the robin do then,
   Poor thing?

He'll sit in a barn,
And keep himself warm,
And hide his head under his wing,
   Poor thing!

I had a little pony,
 His name was Dapple-gray,
I lent him to a lady,
 To ride a mile away;
She whipped him, she lashed him,
 She rode him through the mire;
I would not lend my pony now
 For all the lady's hire.

I had a little doggy that used to sit and beg;
But Doggy tumbled down the stairs and broke
 his little leg.
Oh! Doggy, I will nurse you, and try to make
 you well,
And you shall have a collar with a little silver
 bell.

Ah! Doggy, don't you think you should very
    faithful be,
For having such a loving friend to comfort you
    as me?
And when your leg is better, and you can run
    and play,
We'll have a scamper in the fields and see them
    making hay.

But, Doggy, you must promise (and mind your
    word you keep)
Not once to tease the little lambs, or run among
    the sheep;
And then the little yellow chicks that play upon
    the grass,
You must not even wag your tail to scare them
    as you pass.

    Pussy sits beside the fire—
      How can she be fair?
    In comes little puppy-dog:
      " Pussy, are you there?
    So, so, Mistress Pussy,
    Pray how do you do? "
    " Thank you, thank you, little dog,
    I'm very well just now."

Baa, baa, black sheep,
   Have you any wool?
Yes, marry, have I,
   Three bags full:

One for my master,
   One for my dame,
And one for the little boy
   Who lives in the lane.

Pussy-cat, pussy-cat,
   Where have you been?
I've been to London
   To look at the Queen
Pussy-cat, pussy-cat,
   What did you there?
I frightened a little mouse
   Under her chair.

Six little mice sat down to spin,
Pussy passed by, and she peeped in.
" What are you at, my little men? "
" Making coats for gentlemen."
" Shall I come in and bite off your threads? "
" No, no, Miss Pussy, you'll snip off our heads."
" Oh, no, I'll not, I'll help you to spin."
" That may be so, but you don't come in! "

Little Robin Redbreast sat upon a tree,
Up went pussy-cat, and down went he;
Down came pussy-cat, and away Robin ran;
Said little Robin Redbreast, " Catch me if you
    can."

Little Robin Redbreast jumped upon a wall,
Pussy-cat jumped after him, and almost got a
    fall;
Little Robin chirped and sang, and what did
    pussy say?
Pussy-cat said naught but " Mew," and Robin
    flew away.

Cushy, cow bonny, let down thy milk,
And I will give thee a gown of silk:
A gown of silk and a silver tee,
If thou wilt let down thy milk to me.

Betty Pringle had a little pig,
Not very little and not very big,
When he was alive he lived in clover,
But now he's dead, and that's all over.
So Billy Pringle he lay down and cried,
And Betty Pringle she lay down and died;

So there was an end of one, two, and three:
    Billy Pringle he,
    Betty Pringle she,
    And the piggy wig*gee*.

Come hither, sweet Robin,
    And be not afraid,
  I would not hurt even a feather;
Come hither, sweet Robin,
    And pick up some bread,
  To feed you this very cold weather.

I don't mean to frighten you,
    Poor little thing,
  And pussy-cat is not behind me;
So hop about pretty,
    And drop down your wing,
  And pick up some crumbs, and don't
    mind me.

Baby's Breakfast

Baby wants his breakfast,
    Oh! what shall I do?
Said the cow, " I'll give him
    Nice fresh milk—moo-*oo*! "

Said the hen " Cut-*dah* cut!
    I have laid an egg
For the Baby's breakfast—
    Take it now, I beg!"

And the buzzing bee said,
    " Here is honey sweet.
Don't you think the Baby
    Would like that to eat?"

Then the baker kindly
    Brought the Baby's bread.
" Breakfast is all ready,"
    Baby's mother said;

" But before the Baby
    Eats his dainty food,
Will he not say ' Thank you!'
    To his friends so good?"

Then the bonny Baby
    Laughed and laughed away.
That was all the " Thank you"
    He knew how to say.

                  Emilie Poulsson.

PART I

THE ROYAL BABY

V

NURSERY HEROES AND HEROINES

V

NURSERY HEROES AND HEROINES

Bobby Shaftoe's gone to sea,
Silver buckles on his knee;
He'll come back and marry me,
    Pretty Bobby Shaftoe.

Bobby Shaftoe's fat and fair,
Combing down his yellow hair;
He's my love for evermair,
    Pretty Bobby Shaftoe.

Tom, he was a piper's son,
He learned to play when he was young,
And all the tune that he could play
Was, " Over the hills and far away,"
Over the hills, and a great way off,
The wind will blow my top-knot off.

Now, Tom with his pipe made such a noise
That he well pleased both the girls and boys,
And they always stopped to hear him play
" Over the hills and far away."

Jack Horner

Jack Horner was a pretty lad,
   Near London he did dwell;
His father's heart he made full glad,
   His mother loved him well.

While little Jack was sweet and young,
   If he by chance should cry,
His mother pretty sonnets sung,
   With a lul-la-lul-la-by,

With such a dainty curious tone,
   As Jack sat on her knee,
That soon, ere he could go alone,
   He sang as well as she.

A pretty boy of curious wit,
   All people spoke his praise,
And in the corner he would sit
   In Christmas holidays.

When friends they did together meet,
   To pass away the time—
Why, little Jack, be sure, would eat
   His Christmas pie in rhyme.

He said, " Jack Horner, in the corner,
   Eats good Christmas pie,
And with his thumbs pulls out the plums,
   And says, ' Good boy am I!' "

Little Tom Tucker
Sings for his supper;
What shall he eat?
White bread and butter.

How shall he cut it
Without e'er a knife?
How shall he be married
Without e'er a wife?

Simple Simon met a pieman,
  Going to the fair;
Says Simple Simon to the pieman,
  " Let me taste your ware."

Says the pieman to Simple Simon,
  " Show me first your penny."
Says Simple Simon to the pieman,
  " Indeed I have not any."

Simple Simon went a-fishing
  For to catch a whale;
But all the water he could find
  Was in his mother's pail!

Jack and Jill went up the hill,
  To fetch a pail of water;
Jack fell down, and broke his crown,
  And Jill came tumbling after.

Up Jack got and home did trot
    As fast as he could caper;
Went to bed to mend his head
    With vinegar and brown paper.

Jill came in and she did grin,
    To see his paper plaster.
Mother, vexed, did whip her next,
    For causing Jack's disaster.

Little Boy Blue, come blow your horn,
The sheep's in the meadow, the cow's in the corn.
Where's the boy that looks after the sheep?
He's under the haycock, fast asleep.

Little Miss Muffet,
    She sat on a tuffet,
Eating of curds and whey;
    There came a great spider,
    And sat down beside her,
Which frightened Miss Muffet away.

Lucy Locket lost her pocket,
    Kitty Fisher found it;
But never a penny was there in't
    Except the binding round it.

My maid Mary
She minds her dairy,
While I go a-hoeing and mowing each morn.
Merrily run the reel
And the little spinning-wheel
While I am singing and mowing my corn.

Bessy Bell and Mary Gray,
They were two bonny lasses:
They built their house upon the lea,
And covered it with rushes.

Bessy kept the garden gate,
And Mary kept the pantry;
Bessy always had to wait,
While Mary lived in plenty.

Mary, Mary, quite contrary,
How does your garden grow?
With cockle-shells and silver bells
And pretty girls all of a-row.

Curly Locks! Curly Locks! wilt thou be mine?
Thou shalt not wash dishes, nor yet feed the
swine,
But sit on a cushion and sew a fine seam,
And feast upon strawberries, sugar, and cream!

Old King Cole
Was a merry old soul,
And a merry old soul was he;
 He called for his pipe,
 And he called for his bowl,
And he called for his fiddlers three.

Every fiddler he had a fine fiddle,
And a very fine fiddle had he;
"Twee tweedle dee, tweedle dee," went the
 fiddlers.
 Oh, there's none so rare,
 As can compare
With King Cole and his fiddlers three.

There was an old woman went up in a basket
 Seventy times as high as the moon;
And where she was going, I could not but ask it,
 For under her arm she carried a broom.
"Old woman, old woman, old woman," said I,
 "Whither, O whither, O whither so high?"
"I'm sweeping the cobwebs off the sky!"
 "Shall I go with thee?" "Ay, by and by."

PART I

THE ROYAL BABY

VI

NURSERY NONSENSE

VI

NURSERY NONSENSE

Old Mother Goose, when
　She wanted to wander,
Would ride through the air
　On a very fine gander.

Mother Goose had a house,
　'T was built in a wood,
Where an owl at the door
　For sentinel stood.

She had a son Jack,
　A plain-looking lad;
He was not very good,
　Nor yet very bad.

She sent him to market,
　A live goose he bought:
" Here! mother," says he,
　" It will not go for nought."

Jack's goose and her gander
　Grew very fond;
They'd both eat together,
　Or swim in one pond.

Jack found one morning,
  As I have been told,
His goose had laid him
  An egg of pure gold.

Jack rode to his mother,
  The news for to tell.
She called him a good boy,
  And said it was well.

Goosey, goosey, gander,
  Where shall I wander?
Upstairs, downstairs,
  And in my lady's chamber.
There I met an old man
  Who would not say his prayers;
I took him by the left leg,
  And threw him downstairs.

I'll tell you a story
About Mary Morey,
  And now my story's begun.
I'll tell you another
About her brother,
  And now my story's done.

The lion and the unicorn
   Were fighting for the crown;
The lion beat the unicorn
   All round about the town.
Some gave them white bread,
   Some gave them brown,
Some gave them plum-cake,
   And sent them out of town.

Three wise men of Gotham,
   Went to sea in a bowl;
If the bowl had been stronger,
   My song had been longer.

There was a crooked man,
   And he went a crooked mile,
He found a crooked sixpence
   Upon a crooked stile:
He bought a crooked cat,
   That caught a crooked mouse—
And they all lived together
   In a little crooked house.

Pussicat, wussicat, with a white foot,
When is your wedding? for I'll come to't.
The beer's to brew, the bread's to bake,
Pussy-cat, pussy-cat, don't be too late.

There was a man in our town,
   And he was wondrous wise,
He jumped into a bramble bush,
   And scratched out both his eyes;
But when he saw his eyes were out,
   With all his might and main,
He jumped into another bush,
   And scratched 'em in again.

Solomon Grundy,
   Born on a Monday,
Christened on Tuesday,
Married on Wednesday,
Took ill on Thursday,
Worse on Friday,
Died on Saturday.
Buried on Sunday,
   This is the end
   Of Solomon Grundy!

Hey! diddle diddle,
   The cat and the fiddle,
The cow jumped over the moon;
   The little dog laughed
   To see such sport,
While the dish ran away with the spoon.

What are little boys made of, made of?
What are little boys made of?
Snips and snails, and puppy-dogs' tails;
And that's what little boys are made of, made of.

What are little girls made of, made of?
What are little girls made of?
Sugar and spice, and all that's nice;
And that's what little girls are made of, made of.

❦

" Come hither, little puppy-dog,
    I'll give you a new collar,
If you will learn to read your book,
    And be a clever scholar."
" No! no! " replied the puppy-dog,
    " I've other fish to fry;
For I must learn to guard your house,
    And bark when thieves come nigh."

With a tingle, tangle titmouse,
    Robin knows great A,
And B, and C, and D, and E,
    F, G, H, I, J, K.

" Come hither, pretty cockatoo,
    Come and learn your letters;
And you shall have a knife and fork
    To eat with, like your betters."

" No! no! " the cockatoo replied,
  " My beak will do as well;
I'd rather eat my victuals thus
  Than go and learn to spell."

　　With a tingle, tangle titmouse,
　　　Robin knows great A,
　　And B, and C, and D, and E,
　　　F, G, H, I, J, K.

" Come hither, little pussy-cat,
  If you'll your grammar study,
I'll give you silver clogs to wear,
  Whene'er the gutter's muddy."
" No! whilst I grammar learn," says puss,
  " Your house will in a trice
Be overrun from top to toe,
  With flocks of rats and mice."

　　With a tingle, tangle titmouse,
　　　Robin knows great A,
　　And B, and C, and D, and E,
　　　F, G, H, I, J, K.

" Come hither, then, good little boy,
  And learn your alphabet,
And you a pair of boots and spurs,
  Like your papa's, shall get."

" Oh yes! I'll learn my alphabet,
   And when I've learned to read,
Perhaps papa will give me, too,
   A pretty long-tailed steed."

    With a tingle, tangle titmouse,
      Robin knows great A,
    And B, and C, and D, and E,
      F, G, H, I, J, K.

Peter White will ne'er go right:
   Would you know the reason why?
He follows his nose where'er he goes,
   And that stands all awry.

    The man in the moon
    Came down too soon,
And asked his way to Norwich:
    He went by the south,
    And burnt his mouth
With eating cold plum-porridge.

Dear, dear! what can the matter be?
Two old women got up in an apple-tree;
One came down,
And the other stayed up till Saturday.

Upon a great black horse-ily
A man came riding cross-ily;
A lady out did come-ily,
Said she, " No one's at home-ily,

" But only little people-y,
Who've gone to bed to sleep-ily."
The rider on his horse-ily
Said to the lady, cross-ily,

" But are they bad or good-ily?
I want it understood-ily."
" Oh, they act bad and bold-ily,
And don't do what they're told-ily."

" Good-by! " said he, " dear Ma'am-ily,
I've nothing for your family."
And scampered off like mouse-ily
Away, way from the house-ily.
        " Mother Goose from Germany."

The Rabbits

Between the hill and the brook, ook, ook,
    Two rabbits sat in the sun, O!
And there they ate the green, green grass,
    Till all the grass was gone, O!

And when they had eaten enough, nough, nough,
   They sat down to have a talk, O!
When there came a man with a gun, gun, gun,
   And fired at them over the walk, O!

But when they found they were sound, ound,
   ound,
   Nor hurt by the gun, gun, gun, O!
They picked themselves up from the ground,
   ound, ound,
   And scampered away like fun, O!
      " Mother Goose from Germany."

The King of France, and four thousand men,
They drew their swords, and put them up again.

     Hickory, dickory, dock,
     The mouse ran up the clock;
      The clock struck one,
      The mouse ran down,
     Hickory, dickory, dock.

     A cat came fiddling
      Out of a barn,
     With a pair of bagpipes
      Under her arm;

She could sing nothing
But fiddle cum fee,
The mouse has married
The bumble-bee;
Pipe, cat; dance, mouse:
We'll have a wedding
At our good house.

There was an old woman who lived in a shoe,
She had so many children she didn't know what
to do;
She gave them some broth without any bread,
She whipped them all soundly and put them to
bed.

There were two birds sat on a stone,
Fa, la, la, la, lal, de;
One flew away, and then there was one,
Fa, la, la, la, lal, de;
The other flew after,
And then there was none,
Fa, la, la, la, lal, de;
And so the poor stone
Was left all alone,
Fa, la, la, la, lal, de.

If all the seas were one sea,
What a *great* sea that would be!
And if all the trees were one tree,
What a *great* tree that would be!
And if all the axes were one axe,
What a *great* axe that would be!
And if all the men were one man,
What a *great* man he would be!
And if the *great* man took the *great* axe,
And cut down the *great* tree,
And let it fall into the *great* sea,
What a splish splash *that* would be!

As Tommy Snooks and Bessy Brooks
  Were walking out one Sunday,
Said Tommy Snooks to Bessy Brooks,
  " To-morrow will be Monday."

Three children sliding on the ice
  Upon a summer's day,
As it fell out they all fell in,
  The rest they ran away.

Now had these children been at home,
  Or sliding on dry ground,
Ten thousand pounds to one penny
  They had not all been drowned.

Ye parents all, that children have,
    And ye that eke have none,
If you would keep them from the grave,
    Pray make them stay at home.

One misty, moisty morning,
    When cloudy was the weather,
I chanced to meet an old man clothed all in
    leather.
He began to compliment, and I began to grin,
    How do you do, and how do you do?
    And how do you do again?

Brave news is come to town;
    Brave news is carried;
Brave news is come to town—
    Jemmy Dawson's married.

First he got a porridge-pot,
    Then he bought a ladle;
Then he got a wife and child,
    And then he bought a cradle.

There was an old man,
And he had a calf,
    And that's half;

He took him out of the stall,
And tied him to the wall,
And that's all.

The man in the wilderness asked me,
How many strawberries grew in the sea?
I answered him as I thought good,
As many as red herrings grew in the wood.

If all the world were apple-pie,
And all the sea were ink,
And all the trees were bread and cheese,
What should we have for drink?

(*First child*). 1. I am a gold lock.
(*Second child*.)   2. I am a gold key.
            1. I am a silver lock.
               2. I am a silver key.
            1. I am a brass lock.
               2. I am a brass key.
            1. I am a lead lock.
               2. I am a lead key.
            1. I am a monk lock.
               2. I am a monk key.

(*First child.*)   1. I went up one pair of stairs.
(*Second child.*)   2. Just like me.
                1. I went up two pair of stairs.
                  2. Just like me.
                1. I went into a room.
                  2. Just like me.
                1. I looked out of a window.
                  2. Just like me.
                1. And there I saw a monkey.
                  2. Just like me.

Girls and boys, come out to play,
The moon doth shine as bright as day;
Leave your supper and leave your sleep,
And come with your playfellows into the street.
Come with a whoop, come with a call,
Come with a good will or not at all.
Up the ladder and down the wall,
A halfpenny roll will serve us all.
You find milk, and I'll find flour,
And we'll have a pudding in half an hour.

          Gay go up and gay go down,
          To ring the bells of London town.

          "Bull's eyes and targets,"
          Say the bells of St. Marg'ret's.

" Brickbats and tiles,"
Say the bells of St. Giles'.

" Halfpence and farthings,"
Say the bells of St. Martin's.

" Oranges and lemons,"
Say the bells of St. Clement's.

" Pancakes and fritters,"
Say the bells of St. Peter's.

" Two sticks and an apple,"
Say the bells at Whitechapel.

" Old Father Baldpate,"
Say the slow bells at Aldgate.

" You owe me ten shillings,"
Say the bells at St. Helen's.

" Pokers and tongs,"
Say the bells at St. John's.

" Kettles and pans,"
Say the bells at St. Ann's.

" When will you pay me? "
Say the bells of Old Bailey.

" When I grow rich,"
Say the bells of Shoreditch.

"Pray when will that be?"
Say the bells of Stepney.

"I'm sure I don't know,"
Says the great bell at Bow.

I saw a ship a-sailing,
A-sailing on the sea;
And it was full of pretty things
For baby and for me.

There were sweetmeats in the cabin,
And apples in the hold;
The sails were made of silk,
And the masts were made of gold.

The four-and-twenty sailors
That stood between the decks,
Were four-and-twenty white mice,
With chains about their necks.

The captain was a duck,
With a packet on his back;
And when the ship began to move,
The captain cried, "Quack, quack!"

There was a butcher cut his thumb,
When it did bleed, then blood did come.

There was a chandler making candle,
When he them stript, he did them handle.

There was a cobbler clouting shoon,
When they mended, they were done.

There was a crow sat on a stone,
When he was gone, then there was none.

There was a horse going to the mill,
When he went on, he stood not still.

There was a lackey ran a race,
When he ran fast, he ran apace.

There was a monkey climbed a tree,
When he fell down, then down fell he.

There was a navy went into Spain,
When it return'd, it came again.

There was an old woman lived under a hill,
And if she's not gone, she lives there still.

PART I

THE ROYAL BABY

VII

NURSERY NOVELS

VII

NURSERY NOVELS

The Courtship, Merry Marriage, and Picnic Dinner of Cock Robin and Jenny Wren

It was a merry time
  When Jenny Wren was young,
So neatly as she danced,
  And so sweetly as she sung,
Robin Redbreast lost his heart:
  He was a gallant bird;
He doft his hat to Jenny,
  And thus to her he said:—

" My dearest Jenny Wren,
  If you will but be mine,
You shall dine on cherry pie,
  ·And drink nice currant wine.
I'll dress you like a Goldfinch,
  Or like a Peacock gay;
So if you'll have me, Jenny,
  Let us appoint the day."

Jenny blushed behind her fan,
  And thus declared her mind:
" Then let it be to-morrow, Bob,
  I take your offer kind—

Cherry pie is very good!
　　So is currant wine!
But I will wear my brown gown,
　　And never dress too fine."

Robin rose up early
　　At the break of day;
He flew to Jenny Wren's house,
　　To sing a roundelay.
He met the Cock and Hen,
　　And bid the Cock declare,
This was his wedding-day
　　With Jenny Wren, the fair.

The Cock then blew his horn,
　　To let the neighbors know,
This was Robin's wedding-day,
　　And they might see the show.
And first came parson Rook,
　　With his spectacles and band,
And one of *Mother Hubbard's* books
　　He held within his hand.

Then followed him the Lark,
　　For he could sweetly sing,
And he was to be clerk
　　At Cock Robin's wedding.

He sung of Robin's love
  For little Jenny Wren;
And when he came unto the end,
  Then he began again.

Then came the bride and bridegroom;
  Quite plainly was she dressed,
And blushed so much, her cheeks were
  As red as Robin's breast.
But Robin cheered her up;
  "My pretty Jen," said he,
"We're going to be married
  And happy we shall be."

The Goldfinch came on next,
  To give away the bride;
The Linnet, being bride's maid,
  Walked by Jenny's side;
And, as she was a-walking,
  She said, "Upon my word,
I think that your Cock Robin
  Is a very pretty bird."

The Bulfinch walked by Robin,
  And thus to him did say,
"Pray, mark, friend Robin Redbreast,
  That Goldfinch, dressed so gay;

What though her gay apparel
    Becomes her very well,
Yet Jenny's modest dress and look
    Must bear away the bell."

The Blackbird and the Thrush,
    And charming Nightingale,
Whose sweet jug sweetly echoes
    Through every grove and dale;
The Sparrow and Tom Tit,
    And many more, were there:
All came to see the wedding
    Of Jenny Wren, the fair.

" O then," says parson Rook,
    " Who gives this maid away? "
" I do," says the Goldfinch,
    " And her fortune I will pay:
Here's a bag of grain of many sorts,
    And other things beside;
Now happy be the bridegroom,
    And happy be the bride! "

" And will you have her, Robin,
    To be your wedded wife? "
" Yes, I will," says Robin,
    " And love her all my life."

" And will you have him, Jenny,
    Your husband now to be? "
" Yes, I will," says Jenny,
    " And love him heartily."

Then on her finger fair
    Cock Robin put the ring;
" You're married now," says Parson Rook,
    While the Lark aloud did sing:
" Happy be the bridegroom,
    And happy be the bride!
And may not man, nor bird, nor beast,
    This happy pair divide."

The birds were asked to dine;
    Not Jenny's friends alone,
But every pretty songster
    That had Cock Robin known.
They had a cherry pie,
    Beside some currant wine,
And every guest brought something,
    That sumptuous they might dine.

Now they all sat or stood
    To eat and to drink;
And every one said what
    He happened to think;

They each took a bumper,
  And drank to the pair:
Cock Robin, the bridegroom,
  And Jenny Wren, the fair.

The dinner-things removed,
  They all began to sing;
And soon they made the place
  Near a mile round to ring
The concert it was fine;
  And every bird tried
Who best could sing for Robin
  And Jenny Wren, the bride.

Then in came the Cuckoo,
  And he made a great rout;
He caught hold of Jenny,
  And pulled her about.
Cock Robin was angry,
  And so was the Sparrow,
Who fetched in a hurry
  His bow and his arrow.

His aim then he took,
  But he took it not right;
His skill was not good,
  Or he shot in a fright;

For the Cuckoo he missed,
  But Cock Robin killed!—
And all the birds mourned
  That his blood was so spilled.

The Death and Burial of Cock Robin

Who killed Cock Robin?
  "I," said the Sparrow,
  "With my bow and arrow,
I killed Cock Robin."

Who saw him die?
  "I," said the Fly,
  "With my little eye,
I saw him die."

Who caught his blood?
  "I," said the Fish,
  "With my little dish,
I caught his blood."

Who'll make his shroud?
  "I," said the Beetle,
  "With my thread and needle,
I'll make his shroud."

Who'll bear the torch?
  " I," said the Linnet,
  " I'll come in a minute,
I'll bear the torch."

Who'll be the clerk?
  " I," said the Lark,
  " I'll say Amen in the dark;
I'll be the clerk."

Who'll dig his grave?
  " I," said the Owl,
  " With my spade and trowel,
I'll dig his grave."

Who'll be the parson?
  " I," said the Rook,
  " With my little book,
I'll be the parson."

Who'll be chief mourner?
  " I," said the Dove,
  " I mourn for my love;
I'll be chief mourner."

Who'll sing his dirge?
  " I," said the Thrush,
  " As I sing in a bush,
I'll sing his dirge."

Who'll bear the pall?
  " We," said the Wren,
    Both the Cock and the Hen;
" We'll bear the pall."

Who'll carry his coffin?
  " I," said the Kite,
  " If it be in the night,
I'll carry his coffin."

Who'll toll the bell?
  " I," said the Bull,
  " Because I can pull,
I'll toll the bell."

All the birds of the air
  Fell to sighing and sobbing
When they heard the bell toll
  For poor Cock Robin.

My dear, do you know,
How a long time ago,
  Two poor little children,
Whose names I don't know,
Were stolen away on a fine summer's day,
And left in a wood, as I've heard people say.

And when it was night,
So sad was their plight!
    The sun it went down,
    And the moon gave no light!
They sobbed and they sighed, and they bitterly
    cried,
And the poor little things, they lay down and
    died.

    And when they were dead,
    The robins so red,
        Brought strawberry-leaves
    And over them spread;
        And all the day long,
        They sung them this song:
" Poor babes in the wood! Poor babes in the
    wood!
Oh don't you remember the babes in the wood? "

❦

The Queen of Hearts, she made some tarts,
    All on a summer's day;
The Knave of Hearts, he stole the tarts,
    And took them clean away.

The King of Hearts called for the tarts,
    And beat the Knave full sore;
The Knave of Hearts brought back the tarts,
    And vowed he'd steal no more.

A little boy and a little girl
    Lived in an alley;
Said the little boy to the little girl,
    " Shall I, oh! shall I? "

Said the little girl to the little boy,
    " What will you do? "
Said the little boy to the little girl,
    " I will kiss you."

When good King Arthur ruled this land,
    He was a goodly king;
He stole three pecks of barley-meal,
    To make a bag-pudding.

A bag-pudding the king did make,
    And stuff'd it well with plums:
And in it put great lumps of fat,
    As big as my two thumbs.

The king and queen did eat thereof,
    And noblemen beside;
And what they could not eat that night,
    The queen next morning fried.

"Little maid, pretty maid, whither goest thou?"
"Down in the meadow to milk my cow."
"Shall I go with thee?" "No, not now;
When I send for thee, then come thou."

Jack Sprat could eat no fat,
   His wife could eat no lean;
And so, betwixt them both, you see,
   They licked the platter clean.

Peter, Peter, pumpkin eater,
Had a wife and couldn't keep her;
He put her in a pumpkin shell
And then he kept her very well.

The little priest of Felton,
The little priest of Felton,
He kill'd a mouse within his house,
And ne'er a one to help him.

Ding, dong, bell,
Pussy's in the well!
Who put her in?—
Little Tommy Lin.

Who pulled her out?—
Big John Strout.
What a naughty boy was that
To drown poor pussy-cat,
Who never did him any harm,
But kill'd the mice in his father's barn.

When I was a bachelor
   I lived by myself;
And all the bread and cheese I got
   I put upon the shelf.

The rats and the mice
   They made such a strife,
I was forced to go to London
   To buy me a wife.

The streets were so bad,
   And the lanes were so narrow,
I was forced to bring my wife home
   In a wheelbarrow.

The wheelbarrow broke,
   And my wife had a fall,
Down came wheelbarrow,
   Little wife and all.

I had a little husband,
  No bigger than my thumb;
I put him in a pint-pot,
  And there I bade him drum.

I bought a little horse,
  That galloped up and down;
I bridled him, and saddled him,
  And sent him out of town.

I gave him little garters,
  To garter up his hose,
And a little handkerchief,
  To wipe his little nose.

Sing a song of sixpence,
  A pocket full of rye;
Four-and-twenty blackbirds
  Baked in a pie;

When the pie was opened
  The birds began to sing;
Was not that a dainty dish
  To set before the King?

The King was in his counting-house,
  Counting out his money;
The Queen was in the parlour,
  Eating bread and honey;

The maid was in the garden
Hanging out the clothes;
When up came a blackbird,
And nipped off her nose.

❦

Little Bo-peep, she lost her sheep,
And can't tell where to find them;
Leave them alone, and they'll come home,
And bring their tails behind them.

Little Bo-peep fell fast asleep,
And dreamed she heard them bleating;
When she awoke she found it a joke,
For they still were all fleeting.

Then up she took her little crook,
Determined for to find them;
She found them indeed, but it made her heart
bleed,
For they'd left their tails behind them!

It happened one day, as Bo-peep did stray,
Unto a meadow hard by—
There she espied their tails side by side,
All hung on a tree to dry.

She heaved a sigh, and wiped her eye,
    And over the hillocks she raced;
And tried what she could, as a shepherdess
        should,
    That each tail should be properly placed.

There was a little man,
    And he had a little gun,
And his bullets were made of lead, lead, lead;
    He went to the brook,
    And he saw a little duck,
And he shot it right through the head, head, head.

He carried it home,
    To his good wife Joan,
And bid her make a fire for to bake, bake, bake,
    To roast the little duck
    He had shot in the brook,
And he'd go fetch her next the drake, drake,
        drake.

The drake had gone to sail,
    With his nice curly tail,
The little man made it his mark, mark, mark.
    But he let off his gun,
    And he fired too soon,
So the drake flew away with a quack, quack,
        quack.

Three little kittens, they lost their mittens,
  And they began to cry,
    O mother dear,
    We very much fear,
  That we have lost our mittens.
  Lost your mittens!
  You naughty kittens!
Then you shall have no pie.
    Mee-ow, mee-ow, mee-ow.
No, you shall have no pie.
    Mee-ow, mee-ow, mee-ow.

The three little kittens, they found their mittens,
  And they began to cry,
    O mother dear,
    See here, see here!
See! we have found our mittens.
  Put on your mittens,
  You silly kittens,
And you may have some pie.
    Purr-r, purr-r, purr-r,
O let us have the pie.
    Purr-r, purr-r, purr-r.

The three little kittens put on their mittens,
  And soon ate up the pie;
    O mother dear,
    We greatly fear,
That we have soiled our mittens.

Soiled your mittens!
You naughty kittens!
Then they began to sigh,
Mee-ow, mee-ow, mee-ow.
Then they began to sigh,
Mee-ow, mee-ow, mee-ow.

The three little kittens, they washed their mittens,
And hung them out to dry;
O mother dear,
Do you not hear,
That we have washed our mittens?
Washed your mittens!
O, you're good kittens.
But I smell a rat close by:
Hush! Hush! *mee-ow, mee-ow.*
We smell a rat close by,
Mee-ow, mee-ow, mee-ow.

This is the house that Jack built.

This is the malt
That lay in the house that Jack built.

This is the rat,
That ate the malt
That lay in the house that Jack built.

This is the cat,
That killed the rat,
That ate the malt
That lay in the house that Jack built.

This is the dog,
That worried the cat,
That killed the rat,
That ate the malt
That lay in the house that Jack built.

This is the cow with the crumpled horn,
That tossed the dog,
That worried the cat,
That killed the rat,
That ate the malt
That lay in the house that Jack built.

This is the maiden all forlorn,
That milked the cow with the crumpled horn,
That tossed the dog,
That worried the cat,
That killed the rat,
That ate the malt
That lay in the house that Jack built.

This is the man all tattered and torn,
That kissed the maiden all forlorn,
That milked the cow with the crumpled horn,

That tossed the dog,
That worried the cat,
That killed the rat,
That ate the malt
That lay in the house that Jack built.

This is the priest all shaven and shorn,
That married the man all tattered and torn,
That kissed the maiden all forlorn,
That milked the cow with the crumpled horn,
That tossed the dog,
That worried the cat,
That killed the rat,
That ate the malt
That lay in the house that Jack built.

This is the cock that crowed in the morn,
That waked the priest all shaven and shorn,
That married the man all tattered and torn,
That kissed the maiden all forlorn,
That milked the cow with the crumpled horn,
That tossed the dog,
That worried the cat,
That killed the rat,
That ate the malt
That lay in the house that Jack built.

This is the farmer sowing his corn,
That kept the cock that crowed in the morn,

That waked the priest all shaven and shorn,
That married the man all tattered and torn,
That kissed the maiden all forlorn,
That milked the cow with the crumpled horn,
That tossed the dog,
That worried the cat,
That killed the rat,
That ate the malt
That lay in the house that Jack built.

This is the key of the kingdom.
In that kingdom there is a city.
In that city there is a town.
In that town there is a street.
In that street there is a lane.
In that lane there is a yard.
In that yard there is a house.
In that house there is a room.
In that room there is a bed.
On that bed there is a basket.
In that basket there are some flowers.
Flowers in the basket, basket in the bed, bed
    in the room, etc., etc.

Tree on the Hill

On yonder hill there stands a tree;
Tree on the hill, and the hill stood still.

And on the tree there was a branch;
Branch on the tree, tree on the hill, and the hill
stood still.

And on the branch there was a nest;
Nest on the branch, branch on the tree, tree on
the hill, and the hill stood still.

And in the nest there was an egg;
Egg in the nest, nest on the branch, branch on
the tree, tree on the hill, and the hill stood
still.

And in the egg there was a bird;
Bird in the egg, egg in the nest, nest on the
branch, branch on the tree, tree on the hill,
and the hill stood still.

And on the bird there was a feather;
Feather on the bird, bird in the egg, egg in the
nest, nest on the branch, branch on the tree,
tree on the hill, and the hill stood still.

John Ball shot them all.

John Scott made the shot,
  But John Ball shot them all.

John Wiming made the priming,
And John Scott made the shot;
  But John Ball shot them all.

John Brammer made the rammer,
And John Wiming made the priming,
And John Scott made the shot,
  But John Ball shot them all.

John Block made the stock,
And John Brammer made the rammer,
And John Wiming made the priming,
And John Scott made the shot;
  But John Ball shot them all.

John Crowder made the powder,
And John Block made the stock,
And John Brammer made the rammer,
And John Wiming made the priming,
And John Scott made the shot;
  But John Ball shot them all.

John Puzzle made the muzzle,
And John Crowder made the powder,

And John Block made the stock,
And John Brammer made the rammer,
And John Wiming made the priming,
And John Scott made the shot;
  But John Ball shot them all.

John Clint made the flint,
And John Puzzle made the muzzle,
And John Crowder made the powder,
And John Block made the stock,
And John Brammer made the rammer,
And John Wiming made the priming,
And John Scott made the shot;
  But John Ball shot them all.

John Patch made the match,
And John Clint made the flint,
And John Puzzle made the muzzle,
And John Crowder made the powder,
And John Block made the stock,
And John Brammer made the rammer,
And John Wiming made the priming,
And John Scott made the shot;
  But John Ball shot them all.

PART I

THE ROYAL BABY

VIII

GUESS-ME-QUICKS

VIII

GUESS-ME-QUICKS

Riddle me, riddle me, riddle me ree,
Perhaps you can tell me what this may be.

In marble walls as white as milk,
Lined with a skin as soft as silk;
Within a fountain crystal clear,
A golden apple doth appear.
No doors there are to this stronghold,
Yet thieves break in and steal the gold.

Thirty white horses upon a red hill,
Now they tramp, now they champ, now they
stand still.

Black within and red without;
Four corners round about.

Little Nan Etticoat,
In a white petticoat,
And a red nose;
The longer she stands,
The shorter she grows.

As round as an apple, as deep as a cup,
And all the King's horses can't pull it up.

Long legs, crooked thighs,
Little head, and no eyes.

Higher than a house, higher than a tree,
Oh, whatever can that be?

Down in a dark dungeon I saw a brave knight,
All saddled, all bridled, all fit for the fight.
Gilt was his saddle, and bent was his bow;
Thrice I've told you his name, and yet you don't
know.

Humpty Dumpty sat on a wall,
Humpty Dumpty had a great fall;
Not all the King's horses, nor all the King's men,
Could set Humpty Dumpty up again.

Elizabeth, Elspeth, Betsy, and Bess,
They all went together to seek a bird's nest.
They found a bird's nest with five eggs in,
They all took one, and left four in.

As soft as silk, as white as milk,
As bitter as gall, a thick wall,
And a green coat covers me all.

As I went through the garden gap,
Whom should I meet but Dick Red-cap!
A stick in his hand, a stone in his throat:
If you'll tell me this riddle, I'll give you a groat.

I went to the wood and got it;
I sat me down and looked at it;
The more I looked at it the less I liked it;
And I brought it home because I couldn't help it.

There was a girl in our town,
Silk an' satin was her gown,
Silk an' satin, gold an' velvet,
Guess her name, three times I've tell'd it.

As I was going to St. Ives
I met a man with seven wives;
Every wife had seven sacks,
Every sack had seven cats,
Every cat had seven kits.
Kits, cats, sacks, and wives,
How many were going to St. Ives?

Two legs sat upon three legs,
With one leg in his lap;
In comes four legs,
And runs away with one leg.
Up jumps two legs,
Catches up three legs,
Throws it after four legs,
And makes him bring back one leg.

As I was going o'er Westminster bridge,
I met with a Westminster scholar;
He pulled off his cap, *an' drew* off his glove,
And wished me a very good morrow.
What is his name?

Flour of England, fruit of Spain,
Met together in a shower of rain;
Put in a bag tied round with a string,
If you'll tell me this riddle, I'll give you a ring.

I had a little nut tree, nothing would it bear
But a silver nutmeg, and a golden pear.
The King of Spain's daughter came to visit me,
And all was because of my little nut tree.
I skipped over water, I danced over sea,
And all the birds of the air, they couldn't catch
    me.

❦

There is one that has a head without an eye,
   And there's one that has an eye without a
    head:
You may find the answer if you try;
   And when all is said,
Half the answer hangs upon a thread!

Christina G. Rossetti.

❦

Do You Guess it is I?

I am a little thing;
   I am not very high;
I laugh, dance and sing,
   And sometimes I cry.

I have a little head
   All covered o'er with hair,
And I hear what is said
   With my two ears there.

On my two feet I walk;
  I run too with ease;
With my little tongue I talk
  Just as much as I please.

I have ten fingers too,
  And just so many toes;
Two eyes to see through,
  And but one little nose.

I've a mouth full of teeth,
  Where my bread and milk go in;
And close by, underneath,
  Is my little round chin.

What is this little thing,
  Not very, very high,
That can laugh, dance and sing?
  Do you guess it is I?

                 Eliza Lee Follen.

PART I

THE ROYAL BABY

IX

GRANDMOTHER'S WISDOM

IX

GRANDMOTHER'S WISDOM

He that would thrive
Must rise at five;
He that hath thriven
May lie till seven;
And he that by the plough would thrive
Himself must either hold or drive.

Cock crows in the morn,
To tell us to rise,
And he who lies late
Will never be wise.
For early to bed,
And early to rise,
Is the way to be healthy
And wealthy and wise.

A swarm of bees in May
Is worth a load of hay;

A swarm of bees in June
Is worth a silver spoon;
A swarm of bees in July
Is not worth a fly.

As the days grow longer
The storms grow stronger.

When the days begin to lengthen
Then the cold begins to strengthen.

A sunshiny shower,
Won't last half an hour.

March winds and April showers
Bring forth May flowers.

Evening red and morning gray
Set the traveller on his way,
But evening gray and morning red,
Bring the rain upon his head.

When Jacky's a very good boy,
  He shall have cakes and a custard;
But when he does nothing but cry,
  He shall have nothing but mustard.

Rainbow at night
Is the sailor's delight;
Rainbow at morning,
Sailors, take warning.

Thirty days hath September,
April, June, and November;
February has twenty-eight alone,
All the rest have thirty-one,
Excepting leap-year, that's the time
When February's days are twenty-nine.

For every ill beneath the sun
There is a cure or there is none;
If there be one, try to find it;
If there be none, never mind it.

They that wash on Monday
  Have all the week to dry;
They that wash on Tuesday
  Are not so much awry;
They that wash on Wednesday
  Are not so much to blame;
They that wash on Thursday
  Wash for very shame;

They that wash on Friday
　Wash because of need;
And they that wash on Saturday,
　Oh, they are lazy indeed!

　　Go to bed first,
　　A golden purse;

　　Go to bed second,
　　A golden pheasant;

　　Go to bed third,
　　A golden bird.

If you sneeze on Monday, you sneeze for dan-
　ger;
Sneeze on a Tuesday, kiss a stranger;
Sneeze on a Wednesday, sneeze for a letter;
Sneeze on a Thursday, something better;
Sneeze on a Friday, sneeze for sorrow;
Sneeze on a Saturday, joy to-morrow.

　　When the wind is in the east,
　　'Tis good for neither man nor beast;
　　When the wind is in the north,
　　The skilful fisher goes not forth;

When the wind is in the south,
It blows the bait in the fishes' mouth;
When the wind is in the west,
Then 'tis at the very best.

Hearts, like doors, will ope with ease
To very, very little keys,
And don't forget that two of these,
Are "I thank you" and "If you please."

If wishes were horses,
    Beggars would ride;
If turnips were watches,
    I'd wear one by my side.

Cross-patch,
Draw the latch,
Sit by the fire and spin;
Take a cup,
And drink it up,
Then call your neighbors in.

For want of a nail, the shoe was lost;
For want of the shoe, the horse was lost;

For want of the horse, the rider was lost;
For want of the rider, the battle was lost;
For want of the battle, the kingdom was lost;
And all from the want of a horseshoe nail.

Monday's child is fair of face,
Tuesday's child is full of grace,
Wednesday's child is full of woe,
Thursday's child has far to go,
Friday's child is loving and giving,
Saturday's child works hard for its living,
But the child that is born on the Sabbath day
Is bonny and blithe, and good and gay.

My Lady Wind, my Lady Wind,
Went round about the house to find
    A chink to set her foot in;
She tried the keyhole in the door,
She tried the crevice in the floor,
    And drove the chimney soot in.

And then one night when it was dark,
She blew up such a tiny spark
    That all the town was bothered;
From it she raised such flame and smoke
That many in great terror woke,
    And many more were smothered.

And thus when once, my little dears,
A whisper reaches itching ears—
   The same will come, you'll find:
Take my advice, restrain the tongue,
Remember what old nurse has sung
   Of busy Lady Wind.

PART II

LITTLE PRINCE AND PRINCESS

I

THE PALACE PLAYTIME

I

THE PALACE PLAYTIME

Follow Me!

Children go
To and fro,
In a merry, pretty row,
Footsteps light,
Faces bright;
'Tis a happy sight,
Swiftly turning round and round,
Never look upon the ground;
Follow me,
Full of glee,
Singing merrily.

Work is done,
Play's begun;
Now we have our laugh and fun;
Happy days,
Pretty plays,
And no naughty ways.
Holding fast each other's hand,
We're a happy little band;

Follow me,
Full of glee,
Singing merrily.

Birds are free;
So are we;
And we live as happily.
Work we do,
Study too,
For we learn " Twice two ";
Then we laugh, and dance, and sing,
Gay as larks upon the wing;
Follow me,
Full of glee,
Singing merrily.

Eliza Lee Follen.

The Baby's Birthday

Come, Charles, blow the trumpet,
And George, beat the drum,
For this is the baby's birthday!
Little Annie shall sing,
And Jemmy shall dance,
And father the jews-harp will play.
Rad-er-er too tan-da-ro te
Rad-er-er tad-or-er tan do re.

Come toss up the ball,
And spin the hum top;
We'll have a grand frolic to-day;
Let's make some soap bubbles,
And blow them up high,
And see what the baby will say.
Rad-er-er too tan-da-ro te
Rad-er-er tad-or-er tan do re.

We'll play the grand Mufti;
Let's all make a ring;
The tallest the Mufti shall play;
You must look in his face,
And see what he does,
And mind what the Mufti shall say.
Rad-er-er too tan-da-ro te
Rad-er-er tad-or-er tan do re.

And now we'll play soldiers;
All hold up your heads!
Don't you know 'tis the baby's birthday?
You must turn out your toes,
And toss your feet high;
There! this, boys and girls, is the way.
Rad-er-er too tan-da-ro te
Rad-er-er tad-or-er tan do re.

Eliza Lee Follen.

Counting Out

Intery, mintery, cutery-corn,
Apple seed and apple thorn;
Wire, brier, limber-lock,
Five geese in a flock,
Sit and sing by a spring,
O-u-t, and in again.

A Tea-Party

You see, merry Phillis, that dear little maid,
   Has invited Belinda to tea;
Her nice little garden is shaded by trees,—
   What pleasanter place could there be?

There's a cake full of plums, there are strawber-
     ries too,
   And the table is set on the green;
I'm fond of a carpet all daisies and grass,—
   Could a prettier picture be seen?

A blackbird (yes, blackbirds delight in warm
     weather,)
   Is flitting from yonder high spray;
He sees the two little ones talking together,—
   No wonder the blackbird is gay.

                   Kate Greenaway.

Around the World

In go-cart so tiny
　My sister I drew;
And I've promised to draw her
　The wide world through.

We have not yet started—
　I own it with sorrow—
Because our trip's always
　Put off till to-morrow.

Kate Greenaway.

My Ship and I *

O it's I that am the captain of a tidy little ship,
　Of a ship that goes a-sailing on the pond;
And my ship it keeps a-turning all around and
　all about;
But when I'm a little older, I shall find the secret
　out
　How to send my vessel sailing on beyond.

For I mean to grow as little as the dolly at the
　helm,
　And the dolly I intend to come alive;

And with him beside to help me, it's a-sailing I
    shall go,
It's a-sailing on the water, when the jolly breezes
    blow
    And the vessel goes a divie-divie-dive.

O it's then you'll see me sailing through the rushes
    and the reeds,
    And you'll hear the water singing at the prow;
For beside the dolly sailor, I'm to voyage and
    explore,
To land upon the island where no dolly was be-
    fore,
    And to fire the penny cannon in the bow.

Robert Louis Stevenson.

The Feast of the Doll

In flow'ry Japan, the home of the fan,
    The land of the parasol,
Each month has its feast, from greatest to least,
    And March is the Feast of the Doll-doll-doll,
    And March is the Feast of the Doll.

The wee, slippered maid in gown of brocade,
    The baby with shaven poll,
The little brown lad in embroidery clad,
    All troop to the Feast of the Doll-doll-doll,
    All troop to the Feast of the Doll.

How pleasant 'twould be, 'neath an almond-tree,
    In sunshine and perfume to loll,
Forget our own spring, with its wind and its
        sting,
    And sing to the praise of the Doll-doll-doll,
    And sing to the praise of the Doll.

Come, sweet Tippytoes, as pink as a rose,
    And white as a cotton-boll;
Let us follow the plan of the folk in Japan,
    And dance for your Feast, little Doll-doll-doll,
    And dance for your Feast, little Doll.

                            Nora Archibald Smith.

Cuddle Down, Dolly

They sent me to bed, dear, so dreadfully early,
I hadn't a moment to talk to my girlie;
But while Nurse is getting her dinner downstairs,
I'll rock you a little and hear you your prayers.
                Cuddle down, dolly,
                Cuddle down, dear!
Here on my shoulder you've nothing to fear.
That's what Mamma sings to me every night,
Cuddle down, dolly dear, shut your eyes tight!

Not comfor'ble dolly?—or why do you fidget?
You're hurting my shoulder, you troublesome
  midget!
Perhaps it's that hole that you told me about.
Why, darling, your sawdust is trick-ker-ling
  out!!

We'll call the good doctor in, right straight
  away;
This can't be neglected a single more day;
I'll wet my new hankchif and tie it round tight,
'Twill keep you from suffering pains in the night.

I hope you've been good, little dolly, to-day,
Not cross to your nursie, nor rude in your play;
Nor dabbled your feet in those puddles of water
The way you did yesterday, bad little daughter!

       .   .   .   .

Oh, dear! I'm so sleepy—can't hold up my head,
I'll sing one more verse, then I'll creep into bed.
           Cuddle down, dolly,
           Here on my arm,
Nothing shall frighten you, nothing shall harm
Cuddle down sweetly, my little pink rose,
Good angels come now and guard thy repose.

                              Kate Douglas Wiggin.

Playgrounds

In summer I am very glad
  We children are so small,
For we can see a thousand things
  That men can't see at all.

They don't know much about the moss
  And all the stones they pass:
They never lie and play among
  The forests in the grass:

They walk about a long way off;
  And, when we're at the sea,
Let father stoop as best he can
  He can't find things like me.

But, when the snow is on the ground
  And all the puddles freeze,
I wish that I were very tall,
  High up above the trees.

            Laurence Alma Tadema.

Keeping Store

We have bags and bags of whitest down
  Out of the milk-weed pods;
We have purple asters in lovely heaps,
  And stacks of golden-rods—

We have needles out of the sweet pine woods,
  And spools of cobweb thread;
We have bachelors' buttons for dolly's dress,
  And hollyhock caps for her head.

                              Mary F. Butts.

One and One *

Two little girls are better than one
Two little boys can double the fun,
Two little birds can build a fine nest,
Two little arms can love mother best.
Two little ponies must go to a span;
Two little pockets has my little man;
Two little eyes to open and close,
Two little ears and one little nose,
Two little elbows, dimpled and sweet,
Two little shoes on two little feet,
Two little lips and one little chin,
Two little cheeks with a rose shut in;
Two little shoulders, chubby and strong,
Two little legs running all day long.
Two little prayers does my darling say,
Twice does he kneel by my side each day,—

* From " Rhymes and Jingles," copyright, 1874, 1904, by Chas.
Scribner's Sons.

Two little folded hands, soft and brown,
Two little eyelids cast meekly down,—
And two little angels guard him in bed,
" One at the foot, and one at the head."

Mary Mapes Dodge.

A Happy Child

My house is red—a little house,
   A happy child am I,
I laugh and play the livelong day,
   I hardly ever cry.

I have a tree, a green, green tree,
   To shade me from the sun;
And under it I often sit,
   When all my work is done.

My little basket I will take,
   And trip into the town;
When next I'm there I'll buy some cake,
   And spend my bright half-crown.

Kate Greenaway.

PART II

LITTLE PRINCE AND PRINCESS

II

THE PALACE GARDEN

II

THE PALACE GARDEN

The Garden Year

January brings the snow,
Makes our feet and fingers glow.

February brings the rain,
Thaws the frozen lake again.

March brings breezes, loud and shrill,
To stir the dancing daffodil.

April brings the primrose sweet,
Scatters daisies at our feet.

May brings flocks of pretty lambs,
Skipping by their fleecy dams.

June brings tulips, lilies, roses,
Fills the children's hands with posies.

Hot July brings cooling showers,
Apricots, and gillyflowers.

August brings the sheaves of corn,
Then the harvest home is borne.

Warm September brings the fruit;
Sportsmen then begin to shoot.

Fresh October brings the pheasant;
Then to gather nuts is pleasant.

Dull November brings the blast;
Then the leaves are whirling fast.

Chill December brings the sleet,
Blazing fire, and Christmas treat.

Unknown.

The Child and the World

I see a nest in a green elm-tree
With little brown sparrows,—one, two, three!
The elm-tree stretches its branches wide,
And the nest is soft and warm inside.
At morn the sun, so golden bright,
Climbs up to fill the world with light;
It opens the flowers, it wakens me,
And wakens the birdies,—one, two, three.
And leaning out of my window high,
I look far up at the blue, blue sky,
And then far out at the earth so green,
And think it the loveliest ever seen,—
The loveliest world that ever was seen!

But by and by, when the sun is low,
And birds and babies sleepy grow,
I peep again from my window high,
And look at the earth and clouds and sky.
The night dew falls in silent showers,
To cool the hearts of thirsty flowers;
The moon comes out,—the slender thing,
A crescent yet, but soon a ring,—
And brings with her one yellow star;
How small it looks, away so far!
But soon, in the heaven's shining blue,
A thousand twinkle and blink at you,
Like a thousand lamps in the sky so blue.

And hush! a light breeze stirs the tree,
And rocks the birdies,—one, two, three.
What a beautiful cradle, that soft, warm nest!
What a dear little coverlid, mother-bird's breast!
She's hugging them close to her, tight, so tight
That each downy head is hid from sight;
But out from under her sheltering wings
Their bright eyes glisten, the darling things!
I lean far out from my window's height
And say, " Dear, lovely world, good-night!
Good-night, dear, pretty, baby moon!
Your cradle you'll outgrow quite soon,
And then, perhaps, all night you'll shine,
A grown-up lady moon, so fine

And bright that all the stars
Will want to light their lamps from yours.
Sleep sweetly, birdies, never fear,
For God is always watching near!
And you, dear, friendly world above,
The same One holds us in His love;
Both you so great, and I so small,
Are safe,—He sees the sparrows fall,
The dear God watcheth over all!"

Kate Douglas Wiggin.

The Gravel Path

Baby mustn't frown,
When she tumbles down;
If the wind should change—Ah me,
What a face her face would be!

Rub away the dirt,
Say she wasn't hurt;
What a world 'twould be—O my,
If all who fell began to cry!

Laurence Alma Tadema.

A Dewdrop

Little drop of dew,
    Like a gem you are;
I believe that you
    Must have been a star.

When the day is bright,
    On the grass you lie;
Tell me then, at night
    Are you in the sky?

                    Frank Dempster Sherman.

Who Has Seen the Wind?

Who has seen the wind?
    Neither I nor you:
But when the leaves hang trembling,
    The wind is passing through.

Who has seen the wind?
    Neither you nor I:
But when the trees bow down their heads,
    The wind is passing by.

                    Christina G. Rossetti

The Wind's Song

O winds that blow across the sea,
  What is the story that you bring?
Leaves clap their hands on every tree
  And birds about their branches sing.

You sing to flowers and trees and birds
  Your sea-songs over all the land.
Could you not stay and whisper words
  A little child might understand?

The roses nod to hear you sing;
  But though I listen all the day,
You never tell me anything
  Of father's ship so far away.

Its masts are taller than the trees;
  Its sails are silver in the sun;
There's not a ship upon the seas
  So beautiful as father's one.

With wings spread out it flies so fast
  It leaves the waves all white with foam.
Just whisper to me, blowing past,
  If you have seen it sailing home.

I feel your breath upon my cheek,
  And in my hair, and on my brow.
Dear winds, if you could only speak,
  I know what you would tell me now.

My father's coming home, you'd say,
  With precious presents, one, two, three;
A shawl for mother, beads for May,
  And eggs and shells for Rob and me.

The winds sing songs where'er they roam;
  The leaves all clap their little hands;
For father's ship is coming home
  With wondrous things from foreign lands.

Gabriel Setoun.

Who Likes the Rain?

" I," said the duck.   " I call it fun,
For I have my pretty red rubbers on;
They make a little three-toed track,
In the soft, cool mud,—quack! quack! "

" I! " cried the dandelion, " I!
My roots are thirsty, my buds are dry."
And she lifted a towsled yellow head
Out of her green and grassy bed.

" I hope 'twill pour! I hope 'twill pour! "
Purred the tree-toad at his gray bark door,
" For, with a broad leaf for a roof,
I am perfectly weather-proof."

Sang the brook: " I laugh at every drop,
And wish they never need to stop
Till a big, big river I grew to be,
And could find my way to the sea."

" I," shouted Ted, " for I can run,
With my high-top boots and rain-coat on,
Through every puddle and runlet and pool
I find on the road to school."

Clara Doty Bates.

Rain *

The rain is raining all around,
    It falls on field and tree,
It rains on the umbrellas here,
    And on the ships at sea.

Robert Louis Stevenson.

*From " Poems and Ballads," copyright, 1895, 1896, by Chas.
Scribner's Sons.*

Rain in Spring

So soft and gentle falls the rain,
You cannot hear it on the pane;
For if it came in pelting showers,
'Twould hurt the budding leaves and flowers.

Gabriel Setoun.

Sun and Rain

If all were rain and never sun,
    No bow could span the hill;
If all were sun and never rain,
    There'd be no rainbow still.

Christina G. Rossetti.

Bees

Bees don't care about the snow;
I can tell you why that's so:

Once I caught a little bee
Who was much too warm for me.

Frank Dempster Sherman.

Annie's Garden

In little Annie's garden
  Grew all sorts of posies;
There were pinks, and mignonette,
  And tulips, and roses.

Sweet peas, and morning glories,
  A bed of violets blue,
And marigolds, and asters,
  In Annie's garden grew.

There the bees went for honey,
  And the humming-birds too;
And there the pretty butterflies
  And the lady-birds flew.

And there among her flowers,
  Every bright and pleasant day,
In her own pretty garden
  Little Annie went to play.
              Eliza Lee Follen.

The Daisy

I'm a pretty little thing,
Always coming with the spring;
In the meadows green I'm found,
Peeping just above the ground;

And my stalk is covered flat
With a white and yellow hat.
Little lady, when you pass
Lightly o'er the tender grass,
Skip about, but do not tread
On my meek and lowly head;
For I always seem to say,
Surely winter's gone away.

Unknown.

Pussy Willow

Pussy Willow wakened
   From her Winter nap,
For the frolic Spring Breeze
   On her door would tap.

" It is chilly weather
   Though the sun feels good;
I will wrap up warmly;
   Wear my furry hood."

Mistress Pussy Willow
   Opened wide her door;
Never had the sunshine
   Seemed so bright before.

Never had the brooklet
   Seemed so full of cheer;

" Good morning, Pussy Willow,
  Welcome to you, dear! "

Never guest was quainter:—
  Pussy came to town
In a hood of silver gray
  And a coat of brown.

Happy little children
  Cried with laugh and shout,
" Spring is coming, coming,
  Pussy Willow's out."

                              Kate L. Brown.

Spring Questions

How do the pussy-willows grow?
How do the meadow violets blow?
How do the brooklet's waters flow?
    Gold-Locks wants to know.

    Long and gray,
    The willows sway,
And the catkins come the first spring day.
    Plenty of them
    On every stem,
    All dressed in fur,
    As if they were
Prepared to keep the cold away.

The violets, too,
In bonnets blue,
And little crooked necks askew,
Stand, sweet and small,
Where the grass is tall,
Content to spy
But a bit of sky,
Nor ever to know the world at all.

The waters run
In shade and sun,
And laugh because the winter's done.
Now swift, now slow,
The pace they go,
Shining between
Their banks of green,
Whither, they neither care nor know.

Clara Doty Bates.

Snowdrops

Great King Sun is out in the cold,
  His babies are sleeping, he misses the fun;
So he knocks at their door with fingers of gold:
  "Time to get up," says Great King Sun.
Though the garden beds are sprinkled with snow,
It's time to get up in the earth below.

Who wakes first? A pale little maid,
    All in her nightgown opens the door,
Peering round as if half afraid
    Before she steps out on the wintry floor.
All in their nightgowns, snowdrops stand,
White little waifs in a lonely land.

Great King Sun with a smile looks down,—
    " Where are your sisters? I want them, too! "
Each baby is hurrying into her gown,
    Purple and saffron, orange and blue,
Great King Sun gives a louder call,—
" Good morning, Papa! " cry the babies all.

W. Graham Robertson.

A Mystery

Flowers from clods of clay and mud!
    Flowers so bright, and grass so green!
Tell me, blade, and leaf, and bud,
    How it is you're all so clean.

If my fingers touch these sods,
    See, they're streaked with sticky earth;
Yet you spring from clayey clods,
    Pure, and fresh, and fair from birth.

Do you wash yourselves at night,
  In a bath of diamond dew,
That you look so fresh and bright
  When the morning dawns on you?

God, perhaps, sends summer showers,
  When the grass grows grey for rain,
To wash the faces of His flowers,
  And bid His fields be green again.

Tell me, blade, and leaf, and bud;
  Flowers so fair, and grass so green,
Growing out of clay and mud,
  How it is you're all so clean.

Gabriel Setoun.

Meadow Talk

"Don't pick all the flowers!" cried Daisy one
    day
To a rosy-cheeked boy who was passing her way;
"If you take every one, you will very soon see
That when next summer comes, not a bud will
    there be!"

    "Quite true!" said the Clover,
    And over and over
    I've sung that same song
    To whoe'er came along."

Quoth the Buttercup, " I
Have not been at all shy
In impressing that rule
On each child of the school."

" I've touched the same subject,"
 Said Timothy Grass.
" ' Leave just a few flowers! '
 I beg, as they pass."

Sighed a shy little Fern,
 From her home in the shade,
" About pulling up roots,
 What a protest I've made! "

" The children are heedless! "
 The Gentian declared,
" When my blossom-time comes,
 Not a bud will be spared."

." Take courage, sweet neighbor! "
 The Violet said;
And raised in entreaty
 Her delicate head.

" The children are thoughtless,
 I own, in my turn;
But if we *all* teach them,
 They cannot but learn."

" The lesson," said the Alders,
  " Is a simple one, indeed,
Where no root is, blooms no flower,
Where no flower is, no seed."

" 'Tis very well said! " chirped the Robin,
  From the elm tree fluttering down;
" If you'll write on your leaves such a lesson,
  I'll distribute them over the town."

" Oh, write it, dear Alders! " the Innocents cried,
  Their pretty eyes tearfully blue;
" You are older than we are; you're strong and
      you're wise—
  There's none but would listen to you! "

  But, ah! the Alders could not write;
    And though the Robin knew
  The art as well as any bird—
    Or so he said—he flew
  Straight up the hill and far away,
    Remarking as he went,
  He had a business errand
    And was not on pleasure bent.

  Did the children learn the lesson,
    Though 'twas never written down?
  We shall know when, gay and blithesome,
    Lady Summer comes to town.
                          Nora Archibald Smith.

Twenty Froggies

Twenty froggies went to school
Down beside a rushy pool.
Twenty little coats of green,
Twenty vests all white and clean.

" We must be in time," said they,
" First we study, then we play ";
That is how we keep the rule,
When we froggies go to school."

Master Bull-frog, brave and stern,
Called his classes in their turn,
Taught them how to nobly strive,
Also how to leap and dive;

Taught them how to dodge a blow,
From the sticks that bad boys throw.
Twenty froggies grew up fast,
Bull-frogs they became at last;

Polished in a high degree,
As each froggie ought to be,
Now they sit on other logs,
Teaching other little frogs.

George Cooper.

The Snail

The Snail he lives in his hard round house,
  In the orchard, under the tree:
Says he, " I have but a single room;
  But it's large enough for me."

The Snail in his little house doth dwell
  All the week from end to end,
You're at home, Master Snail; that's all very
    well,
  But you never receive a friend.

Unknown.

The Worm

No, little worm, you need not slip
Into your hole, with such a skip;
Drawing the gravel as you glide
On to your smooth and slimy side.
I'm not a crow, poor worm, not I,
Peeping about your holes to spy,
And fly away with you in air,
To give my young ones each a share.
No, and I'm not a rolling-stone,
Creaking along with hollow groan;

Nor am I of the naughty crew,
Who don't care what poor worms go through,
But trample on them as they lie,
Rather than pass them gently by;
Or keep them dangling on a hook,
Choked in a dismal pond or brook,
Till some poor fish comes swimming past,
And finishes their pain at last.

For my part, I could never bear
Your tender flesh to hack and tear,
Forgetting that poor worms endure
As much as I should, to be sure,
If any giant should come and jump
On to my back, and kill me plump,
Or run my heart through with a scythe,
And think it fun to see me writhe!

O no, I'm only looking about,
To see you wriggle in and out,
And drawing together your slimy rings,
Instead of feet, like other things:
So, little worm, don't slide and slip
Into your hole, with such a skip.

                                    Ann Taylor.

The City Mouse and the Garden Mouse

The city mouse lives in a house;—
   The garden mouse lives in a bower,
He's friendly with the frogs and toads,
   And sees the pretty plants in flower.

The city mouse eats bread and cheese;—
   The garden mouse eats what he can;
We will not grudge him seeds and stocks,
   Poor little timid furry man.

                    Christina G. Rossetti.

The Robin to His Mate

Said Robin to his pretty mate,
   " Bring here a little hay;
Lay here a stick and there a straw,
   And bring a little clay.

" And we will build a little nest,
   Wherein you soon shall lay
Your little eggs, so smooth, so blue;
   Come, let us work away.

" And you shall keep them very warm;
   And only think, my dear,
'Twill not be long before we see
   Four little robins here.

" They'll open wide their yellow mouths,
  And we will feed them well;
For we shall love the little dears,
  Oh, more than I can tell!

" And while the sun is shining warm
  Up in the summer sky,
I'll sit and sing to them and you,
  Up in the branches high.

" And all night long, my love, you'll sit
  Upon the pretty nest,
And keep the little robins warm
  Beneath your downy breast."

Mrs. Carter.

The Brown Thrush

There's a merry brown thrush sitting up in the
    tree.
He's singing to me! He's singing to me!
  And what does he say, little girl, little boy?
  "Oh, the world's running over with joy!
        Don't you hear? Don't you see?
        Hush! Look! In my tree,
        I'm as happy as happy can be! "

And the brown thrush keeps singing, " A nest do
    you see
And five eggs, hid by me in the juniper tree?
  Don't meddle! Don't touch! little girl, little
    boy,
    Or the world will lose some of its joy!
      Now I'm glad! now I'm free!
      And I always shall be,
      If you never bring sorrow to me."

So the merry brown thrush sings away in the tree,
To you and to me, to you and to me;
  And he sings all the day, little girl, little boy,
  " Oh, the world's running over with joy!
      But long it won't be,
      Don't you know? Don't you see?
      Unless we're as good as can be."

Lucy Larcom.

The Little Doves

High on the top of an old pine-tree,
Broods a mother dove with her young ones three;
Warm over them is her soft downy breast,
And they sing so sweetly in their nest:
" Coo," say the little ones, " Coo," says she,
All in their nest in the old pine-tree.

Soundly they sleep through the moonshiny night,
Each young one covered and tucked in tight;
Morn wakes them up with the first blush of light,
And they sing to each other with all their might:
" Coo," say the little ones, " Coo," says she,
All in their nest in the old pine-tree.

When in the nest they are all left alone,
While their mother dear for their food has flown,
Quiet and gentle they all remain,
Till their mother they see come home again:
Then " Coo," say the little ones, " Coo," says she,
All in their nest in the old pine-tree.

When they are fed by their tender mother,
One never will push nor crowd another:
Each opens widely his own little bill,
And he patiently waits, and gets his fill:
Then " Coo," say the little ones, " Coo," says she,
All in their nest in the old pine-tree.

Wisely the mother begins, by and by,
To make her young ones learn to fly;
Just for a little way over the brink,
Then back to the nest as quick as a wink:
And " Coo," say the little ones, " Coo," says she,
All in their nest in the old pine-tree.

Fast grow the young ones, day and night,
Till their wings are plumed for a longer flight;
Till unto them at the last draws nigh
The time when they all must say good-by:
Then " Coo," say the little ones, " Coo," says she,
And away they fly from the old pine-tree.

                                        Unknown.

The Other Side of the Sky

A pool in a garden green,
    And the sky hung over all;
Down to the water we lean—
    What if I let you fall?

A little splash and a cry,
    A little gap in the blue,
And you'd fall right into the sky—
    Into the sky—and through.

What do you think they'd think?
    How do you think they'd greet
A little wet baby in pink
    Tumbling down at their feet?

I wonder if they'd be shy,
    Those folk of the Far Away:
On the other side of the Sky,
    Do you think you'd be asked to stay?

I think they would say—" No, no "
   (Peeping down through a crack),
" For they seem to want her below,
   And so we must send her back."
W. Graham Robertson.

The Happy World

The bee is a rover;
   The brown bee is gay;
To feed on the clover,
   He passes this way.
Brown bee, humming over,
   What is it you say?
" The world is so happy—so happy to-day! "

The martens have nested
   All under the eaves;
The field-mice have jested
   And played in the sheaves;
We have played, too, and rested,
   And none of us grieves,
All over the wide world, who is it that grieves?
William Brighty Rands.

Come, Little Leaves

" Come, little leaves," said the wind one day.
" Come over the meadows with me and play;
Put on your dresses of red and gold,
For summer is gone and the days grow cold."

Soon as the leaves heard the wind's loud call,
Down they came fluttering, one and all;
Over the brown fields they danced and flew,
Singing the sweet little song they knew.

" Cricket, good-by, we've been friends so long,
Little brook, sing us your farewell song;
Say you are sorry to see us go;
Ah, you will miss us, right well we know.

" Dear little lambs in your fleecy fold,
Mother will keep you from harm and cold;
Fondly we watched you in vale and glade,
Say, will you dream of our loving shade? "

Dancing and whirling, the little leaves went,
Winter had called them, and they were content;
Soon, fast asleep in their earthy beds,
The snow laid a coverlid over their heads.

George Cooper.

Little Jack Frost

Little Jack Frost went up the hill,
Watching the stars and the moon so still,
Watching the stars and the moon so bright,
And laughing aloud with all his might.
Little Jack Frost ran down the hill,
Late in the night when the winds were still,
Late in the fall when the leaves fell down,
Red and yellow and faded brown.

Little Jack Frost walked through the trees,
" Ah," sighed the flowers, " we freeze, we freeze."
" Ah," sighed the grasses, " we die, we die."
Said Little Jack Frost, " Good-by, Good-by."
Little Jack Frost tripped 'round and 'round,
Spreading white snow on the frozen ground,
Nipping the breezes, icing the streams,
Chilling the warmth of the sun's bright beams.

But when Dame Nature brought back the spring,
Brought back the birds to chirp and sing,
Melted the snow and warmed the sky,
Little Jack Frost went pouting by.
The flowers opened their eyes of blue,
Green buds peeped out and grasses grew;
It was so warm and scorched him so,
Little Jack Frost was glad to go.

                                        Unknown.

The Snow-Bird's Song.

The ground was all covered with snow one day,
And two little sisters were busy at play,
When a snow-bird was sitting close by on a tree,
And merrily singing his chick-a-de-dee,
  Chick-a-de-dee, chick-a-de-dee,
  And merrily singing his chick-a-de-dee.

He had not been singing that tune very long
Ere Emily heard him, so loud was his song;
" Oh, sister, look out of the window," said she;
" Here's a dear little bird singing chick-a-de-dee,
  Chick-a-de-dee, etc.

" Oh, mother, do get him some stockings and
  shoes,
And a nice little frock, and a hat, if he choose;
I wish he'd come into the parlor and see
How warm we would make him, poor chick-a-de-
  dee,
  Chick-a-de-dee," etc.

" There is One, my dear child, though I cannot
  tell who,
Has clothed me already, and warm enough too.
Good-morning! Oh, who are as happy as we?"
And away he went singing his chick-a-de-dee.
  Chick-a-de-dee, etc. F. C. Woodworth.

Snow

O come to the garden, dear brother, and see,
   What mischief was done in the night;
The snow has quite covered the nice apple-tree,
   And the bushes are sprinkled with white.

The spring in the grove is beginning to freeze,
   The pond is hard frozen all o'er;
Long icicles hang in bright rows from the trees,
   And drop in odd shapes from the door.

The old mossy thatch, and the meadows so green,
   Are covered all over with white;
The snowdrop and crocus no more can be seen,
   The thick snow has covered them quite.

And see the poor birds how they fly to and fro,
   They're come for their breakfast again;
But the little worms all are hid under the snow,
   They hop about chirping in vain.

Then open the window, I'll throw them some
   bread,
   I've some of my breakfast to spare:
I wish they would come to my hand to be fed,
   But they're all flown away, I declare.

Nay, now, pretty birds, don't be frightened, I
    pray,
  You shall not be hurt, I'll engage;
I'm not come to catch you and force you away,
  And fasten you up in a cage.

I wish you could know you've no cause for alarm,
  From me you have nothing to fear;
Why, my little fingers could do you no harm,
  Although you came ever so near.

Jane Taylor.

PART II

LITTLE PRINCE AND PRINCESS

III

THE PALACE PETS

III

THE PALACE PETS

The Cow *

The friendly cow all red and white,
  I love with all my heart:
She gives me cream with all her might,
  To eat with apple-tart.

She wanders lowing here and there,
  And yet she cannot stray,
All in the pleasant open air,
  The pleasant light of day;

And blown by all the winds that pass
  And wet with all the showers,
She walks among the meadow grass
  And eats the meadow flowers.

Robert Louis Stevenson

The Good Moolly Cow

Come! supper is ready;
  Come! boys and girls, now,

For here is fresh milk
  From the good moolly cow.

Have done with your fife,
  And your row de dow dow,
And taste this sweet milk
  From the good moolly cow

Whoever is fretting
  Must clear up his brow,
Or he'll have no milk
  From the good moolly cow.

And here is Miss Pussy;
  She means by *mee-ow,*
Give me, too, some milk
  From the good moolly cow.

When children are hungry,
  O, who can tell how
They love the fresh milk
  From the good moolly cow!

So, when you meet moolly,
  Just say, with a bow,
" Thank you for your milk,
  Mrs. Good Moolly Cow."
                    Eliza Lee Follen.

The Cow

"Pretty Moo-cow, will you tell
Why you like the fields so well?
You never pluck the daisies white,
Nor look up to the sky so bright;
So tell me, Moo-cow, tell me true,
Are you happy when you moo?"

"I do not pluck the daisies white;
I care not for the sky so bright;
But all day long I lie and eat
Pleasant grass, so fresh and sweet,—
Grass that makes nice milk for you;
So I am happy when I moo."

Mrs. Motherly.

Bossy and the Daisy

Right up into Bossy's eyes,
    Looked the Daisy, boldly,
But, alas! to his surprise,
    Bossy ate him, coldly!

Listen! Daisies in the fields,
    Hide away from Bossy!
Daisies make the milk she yields,
    And her coat grow glossy.

So, each day, she tries to find
  Daisies nodding sweetly,
And although it's most unkind,
  Bites their heads off, neatly!
                    Margaret Deland.

The Clucking Hen

"Will you take a walk with me,
  My little wife, to-day?
There's barley in the barley-field,
  And hay-seed in the hay."

"Thank you," said the clucking hen;
  "I've something else to do;
I'm busy sitting on my eggs,
  I cannot walk with you."

"Cluck, cluck, cluck, cluck,"
  Said the clucking hen;
"My little chicks will soon be hatched,
  I'll think about it then."

The clucking hen sat on her nest,
  She made it in the hay;
And warm and snug beneath her breast,
  A dozen white eggs lay.

Crack, crack, went all the eggs,
　　Out dropt the chickens small!
"Cluck," said the clucking hen,
　　"Now I have you all."

"Come along, my little chicks,
　　I'll take a walk with *you*."
"Hollo!" said the barn-door cock,
　　"Cock-a-doodle-do!"

Aunt Effie's Rhymes.

Chickens in Trouble

"O mother, mother! I'm so cold!"
　　One little chicken grumbled.
"And, mother!" cried a second chick,
　　"Against a stone I've stumbled."

"And oh! I am so sleepy now,"
　　Another chick was moaning;
While chicken fourth of tired wings,
　　Kept up a constant groaning.

"And, mother! I have such a pain!"
　　Peeped out the chicken baby;
"That yellow meal did taste so good,
　　I've eaten too much, may be."

" And there's a black, black cloud up there,"
　Cried all in fear and wonder;
" O mother dear, do spread your wings
　And let us all creep under."

" There, there, my little dears, come here;
　Your cries are quite distressing,"
The mother called, and spread her wings
　For comfort and caressing.

And soon beneath her feathers warm,
　The little chicks were huddled;
" I know what ailed you all," she said,
" You wanted to be cuddled."

And as they nestled cosily
　And hushed their weak complaining,
She told them that the black, black cloud
　Was quite too small for raining.

And one by one they all were soothed,
　And out again went straying,
Until five happy little chicks
　Were in the farmyard playing.

Emilie Poulsson.

From the Norwegian.

The Funniest Thing in the World *

The funniest thing in the world, I know,
Is watchin' the monkeys 'at's in the show!—
Jumpin' and' runnin' an' racin' roun',
'Way up the top o' the pole; nen down!
First they're here, an' nen they're there,
An' ist a'most any an' ever'where!—
Screechin' an' scratchin' wherever they go,
They're the funniest thing in the world, I know!

They're the funniest thing in the world, I
    think:—
Funny to watch 'em eat an' drink;
Funny to watch 'em a-watchin' us,
An' actin' 'most like grown folks does!—
Funny to watch 'em p'tend to be
Skeerd at their tail 'at they happen to see;—
But the funniest thing in the world they do
Is never to laugh, like me an' you!

                  James Whitcomb Riley.

The Orphan's Song

I had a little bird,
    I took it from the nest;
I prest it and blest it,
    And nurst it in my breast.

* From "Rhymes of Childhood," copyright 1902, used by special permission of the publishers, The Bobbs-Merrill Company.

I set it on the ground,
Danced round and round,
And sang about it so cheerly,
  With " Hey, my little bird,
  And ho! my little bird,
And oh! but I love thee dearly!"

I make a little feast
  Of food soft and sweet,
I hold it in my breast,
  And coax it to eat;

I pit, and I pat,
I call this and that,
And I sing about so cheerly,
  With " Hey, my little bird,
  And ho! my little bird,
And ho! but I love thee dearly!"

Sydney Dobell.

The Darling Birds

The darling birds are warm;
  Yes, feather on feather,
  All close together,
The darling birds are warm.
  They care not whether
  'Tis stormy weather,

For they are safe from harm.
With feather on feather,
Tho' 'tis stormy weather,
The darling birds are warm.

                        Unknown.

The Lamb

Now, Lamb, no longer naughty be,
Be good and homewards come with me,
Or else upon another day
You shall not with the daisies play.

Did we not bring you, for a treat,
In the green grass to frisk your feet?
And when we must go home again
You pull your ribbon and complain.

So, little Lamb, be good once more,
And give your naughty tempers o'er.
Then you again shall dine and sup
On daisy white and buttercup.

               Kate Greenaway.

Four Pets

Pussy has a whiskered face,
Kitty has such pretty ways,
Doggie scampers when I call,
And has a heart to love us all.

The dog lies in his kennel,
   And Puss purrs on the rug,
And baby perches on my knee
   For me to love and hug.

Pat the dog and stroke the cat,
   Each in its degree;
And cuddle and kiss my baby,
   And baby dear kiss me.
                Christina G. Rossetti.

A Puppy's Problem

When Midget was a puppy,
   And to the farm was brought,
She found that there were many things
   A puppy must be taught.

Her mother oft had told her
   The first thing to be known
Was how to gnaw and bite, and thus
   Enjoy a toothsome bone.

So Midget practiced biting
  On everything around,
But that was not approved at all,
  To her surprise, she found.

The farmer spoke severely,
  Till Midget shook with fright;
The children shouted " No, no, no!
  Bad Midget! Mustn't bite! "

'Twas just the same with barking;
  At first they all said " Hark! "
Whenever Midget tried her voice;
  " Good puppy! that's it! Bark! "

But then, as soon as Midget
  Could sound a sharp " Bow-wow! "
Alas! the talk was changed to " Hush!
  Such noise we can't allow."

Now wasn't that a puzzle?
  It seemed a problem dark,
That it was right and wrong to bite
  And right and wrong to bark.

A puppy's hardest lesson
  Is when to bark and bite;
But Midget learned it, and became
  A comfort and delight.

                              Emilie Poulsson.

I Like Little Pussy

I like little Pussy,
  Her coat is so warm;
And if I don't hurt her
  She'll do me no harm.
So I'll not pull her tail,
  Nor drive her away,
But Pussy and I
  Very gently will play;
She shall sit by my side,
  And I'll give her some food;
And she'll love me because
  I am gentle and good.

I'll pat little Pussy,
  And then she will purr,
And thus show her thanks
  For my kindness to her;
I'll not pinch her ears,
  Nor tread on her paw,
Lest I should provoke her
  To use her sharp claw;
I never will vex her,
  Nor make her displeased,
For Pussy can't bear
  To be worried or teased.

                    Jane Taylor.

PART II

LITTLE PRINCE AND PRINCESS

IV

THE PALACE JEST-BOOK

IV

THE PALACE JEST-BOOK

The Owl and the Eel and the Warming-Pan

The owl and the eel and the warming-pan,
They went to call on the soap-fat man.
The soap-fat man he was not within:
He'd gone for a ride on his rolling-pin.
So they all came back by the way of the town,
And turned the meeting-house upside down.

                    Laura E. Richards.

The Fastidious Serpent

There was a snake that dwelt in Skye,
    Over the misty sea, oh;
He liv'd upon nothing but gooseberry-pie
    For breakfast, dinner, and tea, oh.

Now gooseberry-pie—as is very well known—
    Over the misty sea, oh,
Is not to be found under every stone,
    Nor yet upon every tree, oh.

173

And being so ill to please with his meat,
 Over the misty sea, oh,
The snake had sometimes nothing to eat,
 And an angry snake was he, oh.

Then he'd flick his tongue and his head he'd
  shake,
 Over the misty sea, oh,
Crying, " Gooseberry-pie! For goodness' sake
 Some gooseberry-pie for me, oh! "

And if gooseberry-pie was not to be had,
 Over the misty sea, oh,
He'd twine and twist like an eel gone mad,
 Or a worm just stung by a bee, oh.

But though he might shout and wriggle about,
 Over the misty sea, oh,
The snake had often to go without
 His breakfast, dinner, and tea, oh.

                              Henry Johnstone.

Snake Story

There was a little Serpent and he wouldn't go
  to school—
 Oh, what a naughty little Snake!

He grinn'd and put his tongue out when they
    said it was the rule—
  Ah, what a naughty face to make.

He wriggled off behind a stone and hid himself
    from sight—
  Oh, what a naughty thing to do!
And went to sleep as if it were the middle of the
    night—
  I wouldn't do like that, would you?

He dreamt of stealing linties' eggs and sucking
    them quite dry—
  Oh, what a greedy thing to dream!
And then he dreamt that he had wings and knew
    the way to fly—
  Ah, what a pleasure that would seem!

By came a collie dog and said, " What have we
    here?
  Oh, it's a horrid little Snake! "
He bark'd at him and woke him up and fill'd him
    full of fear—
  Ah, how his heart began to quake!

How the Serpent got away he really didn't
    know—
  Oh, what a dreadful fright he got!

But he hurried all the way to school as hard as
    he could go,
  Dusty and terrified and hot.

As into school he wriggled, they were putting
    books away—
  " Oh," says the master, " is it you?
Stand upon that stool, sir, while the others go
    to play;
  That's what a truant has to do."

Henry Johnstone.

The Melancholy Pig

  There was a Pig, that sat alone,
    Beside a ruined Pump.
  By day and night he made his moan:
  It would have stirred a heart of stone
  To see him wring his hoofs and groan,
    Because he could not jump.

Lewis Carroll.

Hospitality

Said a Snake to a Frog with a wrinkled skin,
" As I notice, dear, that your dress is thin,
And a rain is coming, I'll take you in."

John B. Tabb.

Lost

"*Lock the dairy door!*"   Oh, hark, the cock is
    crowing proudly!
"*Lock the dairy door!*" and all the hens are
    cackling loudly:
"*Chickle, chackle, chee,*" they cry; "*we haven't
    got the key,*" they cry;
"*Chickle, chackle, chee! Oh, dear, wherever can
    it be!*" they cry.

Up and down the garden walks where all the
    flowers are blowing,
Out about the golden fields where tall the wheat
    is growing,
Through the barn and up the road they cackle
    and they chatter:
Cry the children, "Hear the hens! Why, what
    can be the matter?"

What scraping and what scratching, what bris-
    tling and what hustling;
The cock stands on the fence, the wind his ruddy
    plumage rustling;
Like a soldier grand he stands, and like a trum-
    pet glorious
Sounds his shout both far and near, imperious
    and victorious.

But to partlets down below, who cannot find the
    key, they hear,
" *Lock the dairy door!* "   That's all his challenge
    says to them, my dear.
Why they had it, how they lost it, must remain
    a mystery;
I that tell you, never heard the first part of the
    history.

But if you will listen, dear, next time the cock
    crows proudly,
" *Lock the dairy door!* " you'll hear him tell the
    biddies loudly:
" *Chickle, chackle, chee,*" they cry; " *we haven't
    got the key!* " they cry;
" *Chickle, chackle, chee!   Oh, dear, wherever can
    it be!* " they cry.

Celia Thaxter.

Extremes *

I

A little boy once played so loud
That the Thunder, up in a thunder-cloud,
Said, " Since *I* can't be heard, why, then,
I'll never, never thunder again! "

* *From " The Book of Joyous Children," copyright 1902, by Chas.
Scribner's Sons.*

II

And a little girl once kept so still
That she heard a fly on the window-sill
Whisper and say to a lady-bird,—
"She's the stilliest child I ever heard!"

James Whitcomb Riley.

❦

The Dream of a Girl Who Lived at Seven-Oaks

Seven sweet singing birds up in a tree;
Seven swift sailing-ships white upon the sea;
Seven bright weather-cocks shining in the sun;
Seven slim race-horses ready for a run;
Seven gold butterflies, flitting overhead;
Seven red roses blowing in a garden bed;
Seven white lilies, with honey bees inside them;
Seven round rainbows with clouds to divide
    them;
Seven pretty little girls with sugar on their lips;
Seven witty little boys, whom everybody tips;
Seven nice fathers, to call little maids joys;
Seven nice mothers, to kiss the little boys;
Seven nights running I dreamt it all plain;
With bread and jam for supper I could dream
    it all again!

William Brighty Rands.

The Dream of a Boy Who Lived at Nine-Elms

Nine grenadiers, with bayonets in their guns;
Nine bakers' baskets, with hot-cross buns;
Nine brown elephants, standing in a row;
Nine new velocipedes, good ones to go;
Nine knickerbocker suits, with buttons all complete;
Nine pair of skates with straps for the feet;
Nine clever conjurors eating hot coals;
Nine sturdy mountaineers leaping on their poles;
Nine little drummer-boys beating on their drums;
Nine fat aldermen sitting on their thumbs;
Nine new knockers to our front door;
Nine new neighbours that I never saw before;
Nine times running I dreamt it all plain;
With bread and cheese for supper I could dream
    it all again!

           William Brighty Rands.

A Little Boy's Pocket

Do you know what's in my pottet?
Such a lot of treasures in it!
Listen now while I bedin it:
Such a lot of sings it holds,
And everysin dats in my pottet,
And when, and where, and how I dot it.

First of all, here's in my pottet
A beauty shell, I pit'd it up:
And here's the handle of a tup
That somebody has broked at tea;
The shell's a hole in it, you see:
Nobody knows dat I dot it,
I teep it safe here in my pottet.
And here's my ball too in my pottet,
And here's my pennies, one, two, free,
That Aunty Mary dave to me,
To-morrow day I'll buy a spade,
When I'm out walking with the maid;
I tant put that here in my pottet!
But I can use it when I've dot it.
Here's some more sings in my pottet,
Here's my lead, and here's my string;
And once I had an iron ring,
But through a hole it lost one day,
And this is what I always say—
A hole's the worst sing in a pottet,
Be sure and mend it when you've dot it.

                              Unknown.

A. *Apple Pie*

a

A was once an apple-pie,
  Pidy,
  Widy,
  Tidy,
  Pidy,
  Nice insidy,
  Apple-pie!

b

B was once a little bear,
  Beary,
  Wary,
  Hairy,
  Beary,
  Taky cary,
  Little bear!

c

C was once a little cake,
  Caky,
  Baky,
  Maky,
  Caky,
  Taky caky,
  Little cake!

d

D was once a little doll,
 Dolly,
 Molly,
 Polly,
 Nolly,
 Nursy dolly,
 Little doll!

e

E was once a little eel,
 Eely,
 Weely,
 Peely,
 Eely,
 Twirly, tweely,
 Little eel!

f

F was once a little fish,
 Fishy,
 Wishy,
 Squishy,
 Fishy,
 In a dishy,
 Little fish!

g

G was once a little goose,
>Goosy,
>Moosy,
>Boosey,
>Goosey,
>Waddly-woosy,
>Little goose!

h

H was once a little hen,
>Henny,
>Chenny,
>Tenny,
>Henny,
>Eggsy-any,
>Little hen?

i

I was once a bottle of ink,
>Inky,
>Dinky,
>Thinky,
>Inky,
>Blacky minky,
>Bottle of ink!

j

J was once a jar of jam,
  Jammy,
  Mammy,
  Clammy,
  Jammy,
 Sweety, swammy,
  Jar of jam!

k

K was once a little kite,
  Kity,
  Whity,
  Flighty,
  Kity,
 Out of sighty,
  Little kite!

l

L was once a little lark,
  Larky,
  Marky,
  Harky,
  Larky,
 In the parky,
  Little lark!

m

M was once a little mouse,
Mousy,
Bousy,
Sousy,
Mousy,
In the housy,
Little mouse!

n

N was once a little needle,
Needly,
Tweedly,
Threedly,
Needly,
Wisky, wheedly,
Little needle!

o

O was once a little owl,
Owly,
Prowly,
Howly,
Owly,
Browny fowly,
Little owl!

p

P was once a little pump,
    Pumpy,
    Slumpy,
    Flumpy,
    Pumpy,
  Dumpy, thumpy,
    Little pump!

q

Q was once a little quail,
    Quaily,
    Faily,
    Daily,
    Quaily,
  Stumpy-taily,
    Little quail!

r

R was once a little rose,
    Rosy,
    Posy,
    Nosy,
    Rosy,
  Blows-y, grows-y,
    Little rose!

s

S was once a little shrimp,
      Shrimpy,
      Nimpy,
      Flimpy,
      Shrimpy,
    Jumpy, jimpy,
    Little shrimp!

t

T was once a little thrush,
      Thrushy,
      Hushy,
      Bushy,
      Thrushy,
    Flitty, flushy,
    Little thrush!

u

U was once a little urn,
      Urny,
      Burny,
      Turny,
      Urny,
    Bubbly, burny,
    Little urn!

V

V was once a little vine,
    Viny,
    Winy,
    Twiny,
    Viny,
    Twisty-twiny,
    Little vine!

w

W was once a whale,
    Whaly,
    Scaly,
    Shaly,
    Whaly,
    Tumbly-taily,
    Mighty whale!

x

X was once a great king Xerxes,
    Xerxy,
    Perxy,
    Turxy,
    Xerxy,
    Linxy, lurxy,
    Great King Xerxes!

y

Y was once a little yew,
  Yewdy,
  Fewdy,
  Crudy,
  Yewdy,
Growdy, grewdy,
  Little yew!

z

Z was once a piece of zinc,
  Tinky,
  Winky,
  Blinky,
  Tinky,
Tinkly minky,
  Piece of zinc!

Edward Lear.

A was an Ant

A was an ant
  Who seldom stood still,
And who made a nice house
  In the side of a hill.

a

Nice little ant!

B was a book
  With a binding of blue,
And pictures and stories
  For me and for you.

b

Nice little book!

C was a cat
Who ran after a rat;
But his courage did fail
When she seized on his tail.

c

Crafty old cat!

D was a duck
  With spots on his back,
Who lived in the water,
  And always said " Quack! "

d

Dear little duck!

E was an elephant,
  Stately and wise:
He had tusks and a trunk,
  And two queer little eyes.

e

Oh, what funny small eyes!

F was a fish
  Who was caught in a net;
But he got out again,
  And is quite alive yet.

f

Lively young fish!

G was a goat
  Who was spotted with brown:
When he did not lie still
  He walked up and down.

g

Good little goat!

H was a hat
  Which was all on one side;
Its crown was too high,
  And its brim was too wide.

h

Oh, what a hat!

I was some ice
So white and so nice,
But which nobody tasted;
And so it was wasted.

i

All that good ice!

J was a jackdaw
  Who hopped up and down
In the principal street
  Of a neighboring town.

j
All through the town!

K was a kite
Which flew out of sight,
  Above houses so high,
  Quite into the sky.

k
Fly away, kite!

L was a light
Which burned all the night,
  And lighted the gloom
  Of a very dark room.

l
Useful nice light!

M was a mill
Which stood on a hill,
  And turned round and round
  With a loud hummy sound.

m
Useful old mill!

N was a net
  Which was thrown in the sea
To catch fish for dinner
  For you and for me.

n

Nice little net!

O was an orange
  So yellow and round:
When it fell off the tree,
  It fell down to the ground.

o

Down to the ground!

P was a pig,
Who was not very big;
  But his tail was too curly,
  And that made him surly.

p

Cross little pig!

Q was a quail
With a very short tail;
  And he fed upon corn
  In the evening and morn.

q

Quaint little quail!

R was a rabbit,
Who had a bad habit
  Of eating the flowers
  In gardens and bowers.

r

  Naughty fat rabbit!

S was the sugar-tongs,
  Nippity-nee,
To take up the sugar
  To put in our tea.

s

  Nippity-nee!

T was a tortoise,
  All yellow and black:
He walked slowly away,
  And he never came back.

t

  Torty never came back!

U was an urn
  All polished and bright,
And full of hot water
  At noon and at night.

u

  Useful old urn!

V was a villa
  Which stood on a hill,
By the side of a river,
  And close to a mill.

v

Nice little villa!

W was a whale
With a very long tail,
  Whose movements were frantic
  Across the Atlantic.

w

Monstrous old whale!

X was King Xerxes,
Who, more than all Turks, is
  Renowned for his fashion
  Of fury and passion.

x

Angry old Xerxes!

Y was a yew,
Which flourished and grew
  By a quiet abode
  Near the side of a road.

y

Dark little yew!

Z was some zinc,
　So shiny and bright,
Which caused you to wink
　In the sun's merry light.

z

Beautiful zinc!
　　　　　　　　Edward Lear.

The Table and the Chair

I

Said the Table to the Chair,
" You can hardly be aware
How I suffer from the heat
And from chilblains on my feet.
If we took a little walk,
We might have a little talk;
Pray let us take the air,"
Said the Table to the Chair.

II

Said the Chair unto the Table,
" Now, you *know* we are not able:
How foolishly you talk,
When you know we *cannot* walk!"

Said the Table with a sigh,
" It can do no harm to try.
I've as many legs as you:
Why can't we walk on two? "

III

So they both went slowly down,
And walked about the town
With a cheerful bumpy sound
As they toddled round and round;
And everybody cried,
As they hastened to their side,
" See! the Table and the Chair
Have come out to take the air! "

IV

But in going down an alley,
To a castle in a valley,
They completely lost their way,
And wandered all the day;
Till, to see them safely back,
They paid a Ducky-quack,
And a Beetle, and a Mouse,
Who took them to their house.

V

Then they whispered to each other,
" O delightful little brother,

What a lovely walk we've taken!
Let us dine on beans and bacon."
So the Ducky and the leetle
Browny-Mousy and the Beetle
Dined, and danced upon their heads
Till they toddled to their beds.

                              Edward Lear.

Feeding the Fairies

Fairies, fairies, come and be fed,
 Come and be fed like hens and cocks;
Hither and thither with delicate tread,
 Flutter around me in fairy flocks.
Come, little fairies, from far and near;
 Come, little fairies, I know you can fly;
Who can be dear if *you* are not dear?
 And who is so fond of a fairy as I?

Fairies, fairies, come if you please,
 Nod your heads and ruffle your wings,
Marching in order or standing at ease,
 Frolicsome fairies are dear little things!
Golden the grain and silver the rice,
 Pleasant the crumbs from Mama's own bread,
Currants pick'd out of the pudding are nice—
 Fairies, fairies, come and be fed!

Hushaby, oh! hushaby, oh!
    Hide by the door—keep very still—
I must be gentle, I must speak low,
    Or frighten the fairies I certainly will.
Fairies are easily frighten'd, I know;
    They are so small, we must pity their fears.
Hushaby, oh! hushaby, oh!
    Coax them and humour them — poor little
      dears!

Fairies, fairies, why don't you come?
    Fairies, fairies, wherefore delay?
In a few minutes I must run home—
    Cross little creatures! you know I can't stay!
See how I scatter your beautiful food—
    Good little fairies would come when I call;
Fairies, fairies, *won't* you be good?
    What is the use of my speaking at all?

                    " Two Friends."

The Fairy

Oh, who is so merry
As the light-hearted fairy?
    He dances and sings
    To the sound of his wings,
With a hey, and a heigh, and a ho!

Oh, who is so merry
As the light-hearted fairy?
  His nectar he sips
  From the primrose's lips,
With a hey, and a heigh, and a ho!

Oh, who is so merry
As the light-hearted fairy?
  His night is the noon,
  And his sun is the moon,
With a hey, and a heigh, and a ho!

                                    Unknown.

LITTLE PRINCE AND PRINCESS

PART II

V

THE QUEEN-MOTHER'S COUNSEL

V

THE QUEEN-MOTHER'S COUNSEL

A Thought *

It is very nice to think
The world is full of meat and drink,
With little children saying grace
In every Christian kind of place.

Robert Louis Stevenson.

Inscription for My Little Son's Silver Plate †

When thou dost eat from off this plate,
I charge thee be thou temperate;
Unto thine elders at the board
Do thou sweet reverence accord;
And, though to dignity inclined,
Unto the serving-folk be kind;
Be ever mindful of the poor,
Nor turn them hungry from the door;
And unto God, for health and food
And all that in thy life is good,
Give thou thy heart in gratitude.

Eugene Field.

* *From "Poems and Ballads," copyright, 1895, 1896, by Chas. Scribner's Sons.*

† *From "The Book of Joyous Children," copyright, 1902, by Chas. Scribner's Sons.*

Praise God

Praise God for wheat, so white and sweet,
    Of which to make our bread!
Praise God for yellow corn, with which
    His waiting world is fed!
Praise God for fish and flesh and fowl
    He gave to men for food!
Praise God for every creature which
    He made and called it good!

Praise God for winter's store of ice,
    Praise God for summer's heat!
Praise God for fruit trees bearing seed,
    " To you it is for meat!"
Praise God for all the bounty
    By which the world is fed!
Praise God, ye children all, to whom
    He gives your daily bread!
                 Unknown.

The Eyes of God

God watches o'er us all the day,
At home, at school, and at our play;
And when the sun has left the skies
He watches with a million eyes.
               Gabriel Setoun.

Kindness to Animals

Little children, never give
Pain to things that feel and live:
Let the gentle robin come
For the crumbs you save at home,—
As his meat you throw along
He'll repay you with a song;
Never hurt the timid hare
Peeping from her green grass lair,
Let her come and sport and play
On the lawn at close of day;
The little lark goes soaring high
To the bright windows of the sky,
Singing as if 'twere always spring,
And fluttering on an untired wing,—
Oh! let him sing his happy song,
Nor do these gentle creatures wrong.

Unknown.

How Doth the Little Busy Bee

How doth the little busy bee
  Improve each shining hour,
And gather honey all the day
  From every opening flow'r!

How skilfully she builds her cell!
　　How neat she spreads the wax!
And labours hard to store it well
　　With the sweet food she makes.

In works of labour or of skill,
　　I would be busy too;
For Satan finds some mischief still
　　For idle hands to do.

In books, or work, or healthful play,
　　Let my first years be past,
That I may give for ev'ry day
　　Some good account at last.
　　　　　　　　　　Isaac Watts.

Deeds of Kindness

Suppose the little cowslip
　　Should hang its golden cup,
And say, " I'm such a tiny flower,
　　I'd better not grow up."
How many a weary traveller
　　Would miss its fragrant smell!
How many a little child would grieve
　　To lose it from the dell!

Suppose the glistening dewdrop
  Upon the grass should say,
" What can a little dewdrop do?
  I'd better roll away."
The blade on which it rested,
  Before the day was done,
Without a drop to moisten it,
  Would wither in the sun.

Suppose the little breezes,
  Upon a summer's day,
Should think themselves too small to cool
  The traveller on his way:
Who would not miss the smallest
  And softest ones that blow,
And think they made a great mistake,
  If they were talking so?

How many deeds of kindness
  A little child may do,
Although it has so little strength,
  And little wisdom too!
It wants a loving spirit,
  Much more than strength, to prove
How many things a child may do
  For others by its love.

                       F. P.

Good Advice

Seldom " can't,"
    Seldom " don't ";
Never " shan't,"
    Never " won't."

        Christina G. Rossetti.

I'll Try

Two Robin Redbreasts built their nest
Within a hollow tree;
The hen sat quietly at home,
The cock sang merrily;
And all the little robins said:
" Wee, wee, wee, wee, wee, wee."

One day the sun was warm and bright,
And shining in the sky,
Cock Robin said: " My little dears,
'Tis time you learned to fly ";
And all the little young ones said:
" I'll try, I'll try, I'll try."

I know a child, and who she is
I'll tell you by and by,
When mother says " Do this," or " that,"

She says " What for? " and " Why? "
She'd be a better child by far
If she would say " I'll try."

Unknown.

Clothes

Although my clothes are fine and gay
   They should not make me vain,
For Nurse can take them all away,
   And put them on again.

Each flower *grows* her pretty gown,
   So does each little weed,
Their dresses are their very own,
   They may be proud indeed!

Abbie Farwell Brown.

A Music Box

I am a little Music Box
   Wound up and made to go,
And play my little living-tune
   The best way that I know.

If I am naughty, cross, or rude
   The music will go wrong,
My little works be tangled up,
   And spoil the pretty song.

I must be very sweet and good
And happy all the day,
And then the little Music Box
In tune will always play.

Abbie Farwell Brown.

If Ever I See

If ever I see,
On bush or tree,
Young birds in their pretty nest,
I must not in play,
Steal the birds away,
To grieve their mother's breast.

My mother, I know,
Would sorrow so,
Should I be stolen away;
So I'll speak to the birds
In my softest words,
Nor hurt them in my play.

And when they can fly
In the bright blue sky,
They'll warble a song to me;
And then if I'm sad
It will make me glad
To think they are happy and free.

Lydia Maria Child.

Employment

Who'll come and play with me here under the
    tree,
  My sisters have left me alone;
My sweet little Sparrow, come hither to me,
  And play with me while they are gone.

O no, little lady, I can't come, indeed,
  I've no time to idle away,
I've got all my dear little children to feed,
  And my nest to new cover with hay.

Pretty Bee, do not buzz about over the flower,
  But come here and play with me, do:
The Sparrow won't come and stay with me an
    hour
  But stay, pretty Bee—will not you?

O no, little lady, for do not you see,
  Those must work who would prosper and
    thrive,
If I play, they would call me a sad idle bee,
  And perhaps turn me out of the hive.

Stop! stop! little Ant—do not run off so fast,
  Wait with me a little and play:
I hope I shall find a companion at last,
  You are not so busy as they.

O no, little lady, I can't stay with you,
   We're not made to play, but to labor:
I always have something or other to do,
   If not for myself, for a neighbor.

What then, have they all some employment but
     me,
   Who lie lounging here like a dunce?
O then, like the Ant, and the Sparrow, and Bee,
   I'll go to my lesson at once.

Jane Taylor.

Stitching

A pocket handkerchief to hem—
   Oh dear, oh dear, oh dear!
How many stitches it will take
   Before it's done, I fear.

Yet set a stitch and then a stitch,
   And stitch and stitch away,
Till stitch by stitch the hem is done—
   And after work is play!

Christina G. Rossetti.

Learning to Play

Upon a tall piano stool
  I have to sit and play
A stupid finger exercise
  For half an hour a day.

They call it " playing," but to me
  It's not a bit of fun.
I *play* when I am out of doors,
  Where I can jump and run.

But Mother says the little birds
  Who sing so nicely now,
Had first to learn, and practice too,
  All sitting on a bough.

And maybe if I practice hard,
  Like them, I too, some day,
Shall make the pretty music sound;
  Then I shall call it " play."

Abbie Farwell Brown.

In Trust *

It's coming, boys,
  It's almost here;
It's coming, girls,
  The grand New Year!

* From "Rhymes and Jingles," copyright, 1874, 1904, by Chas. Scribner's Sons.

A year to be glad in,
Not to be bad in;
A year to live in,
To gain and give in;
A year for trying,
And not for sighing;
A year for striving
And hearty thriving;
A bright new year.
Oh! hold it dear;
For God who sendeth
He only lendeth.

Mary Mapes Dodge.

PART II

LITTLE PRINCE AND PRINCESS

VI

THE PALACE BED-TIME

VI

THE PALACE BED-TIME

Watching Angels

Angels at the foot,
  And Angels at the head,
And like a curly little lamb
  My pretty babe in bed.

Christina G. Rossetti.

The Story of Baby's Blanket

Once a little Baby,
  On a sunny day,
Out among the daisies
  Took his happy way.
Little lambs were frisking
  In the fields so green,
While the fleecy mothers
  All at rest were seen.

For a while the Baby
  Played and played and played;
Then he sat and rested
  In the pleasant shade.

Soon a Sheep came near him,
  Growing very bold,
And this wondrous story
  To the Baby told:

" Baby's little blanket,
  Socks and worsted ball,
Winter cap and mittens,
  And his flannels all,
And his pretty afghan
  Warm and soft and fine,
Once as wool were growing
  On this back of mine!

" And the soft bed blankets,
  For his cosey sleep,
These were also given
  By his friends, the sheep."
Such the wondrous story
  That the Baby heard:
Did he understand it?
  Not a single word!

                    Emilie Poulsson.

The Story of Baby's Pillow

These are the Eggs that were put in a nest;
These are the Goslings in yellow down drest.

This is the Farmyard where, living in peace,
All the young Goslings grew up to be Geese.

Here's the Goose family waddling about—
In a procession they always walk out.

This is the Farmer who said, " Every Goose
Now has some feathers on, ready for use."

This is the Farmer's Wife, plucking with care
All of the feathers the Geese can well spare.

This is the Pillow the Merchant displayed:
" Yes, of the finest Goose-feathers 'tis made."

This is the Mother who put on its case,
Laid the wee Pillow away in its place.

This is the Crib with its furnishings white,
This the dear Baby who bids you " Good-night."

Emilie Poulsson.

The New Moon

> Dear mother, how pretty
> The moon looks to-night!
> She was never so cunning before;
> Her two little horns
> Are so sharp and so bright,
> I hope she'll not grow any more.

PINAFORE PALACE

If I were up there
With you and my friends,
I'd rock in it nicely, you see;
I'd sit in the middle
And hold by both ends;
O, what a bright cradle 'twould be!

I would call to the stars
To keep out of the way,
Lest we should rock over their toes,
And there I would rock
Till the dawn of the day,
And see where the pretty moon goes.

And there we would stay
In the beautiful skies,
And through the bright clouds we would roam;
We would see the sun set,
And see the sun rise,
And on the next rainbow come home.

Eliza Lee Follen.

Lady Moon

Lady moon, lady moon,
Sailing so high!
Drop down to baby
From out the clear sky;

Babykin, babykin,
  Down far below,
I hear thee calling,
  But I cannot go.

But lady moon sendeth thee
  Soft shining rays;
Moon loves the baby,
  The moonlight says.
In her house dark and blue,
  Though she must stay,
Kindly she'll watch thee
  Till dawns the new day.

Kate Kellogg.

The Star

Twinkle, twinkle, little star,
How I wonder what you are!
Up above the world so high,
Like a diamond in the sky.

When the blazing sun is gone,
When he nothing shines upon,
Then you show your little light,
Twinkle, twinkle, all the night.

Then the traveller in the dark
Thanks you for your tiny spark:

He could not see which way to go,
If you did not twinkle so.

In the dark-blue sky you keep,
And often through my curtains peep,
For you never shut your eye
Till the sun is in the sky.

As your bright and tiny spark
Lights the traveller in the dark,
Though I know not what you are,
Twinkle, twinkle, little star.

Unknown.

The Child's Star

The star that watched above your sleep has just
    put out his light.
" Good day, to you on earth," he said, " is here in
    heav'n, good night."
" But tell the child when he awakes, to watch for
    my return,
For I'll hang out my lamp again, when his be
    gins to burn."

John B. Tabb.

Do You Know How Many Stars?

Do you know how many stars
There are shining in the skies?

Do you know how many clouds
Ev'ry day go floating by?
God in heaven has counted all,
He would miss one should it fall.

Do you know how many children
Go to little beds at night,
And without a care or sorrow,
Wake up in the morning light?
God in heaven each name can tell,
Loves you, too, and loves you well.

From the German.

Where Do All the Daisies Go?

Where do all the daisies go?
        I know, I know!
Underneath the snow they creep,
Nod their little heads and sleep,
In the springtime out they peep;
        That is where they go!

Where do all the birdies go?
        I know, I know!
Far away from winter snow
To the fair, warm South they go;
There they stay till daisies blow,
        That is where they go!

Where do all the babies go?
  I know, I know!
In the glancing firelight warm,
Safely sheltered from all harm,
Soft they lie on mother's arm,
  That is where they go!

Unknown.

The Sweetest Place

A meadow for the little lambs;
  A honey hive for bees;
And pretty nests for singing birds
  Among the leafy trees.
There's rest for all the little ones
  In one place or another;
But who has half so sweet a place
  As baby with her mother?

The little chickens cuddle close,
  Beneath the old hen's wing;
"Peep! Peep!" they say; "we're not afraid
  Of dark or any thing."
So, safe and sound, they nestle there,
  The one beside the other;
But safer, happier, by far,
  Is baby with her mother.

Mary F. Butts.

Good-Night

Little baby, lay your head
On your pretty cradle-bed;
Shut your eye-peeps, now the day
And the light are gone away;
All the clothes are tucked in tight;
Little baby dear, good-night.

Yes, my darling, well I know
How the bitter wind doth blow;
And the winter's snow and rain
Patter on the window-pane:
But they cannot come in here,
To my little baby dear;

For the window shutteth fast,
Till the stormy night is past;
And the curtains warm are spread
Round about her cradle-bed:
So till morning shineth bright,
Little baby dear, good-night.

                                    Jane Taylor.

Nursery Song

As I walked over the hill one day,
I listened, and heard a mother-sheep say,
" In all the green world there is nothing so sweet
As my little lamb, with his nimble feet;
With his eye so bright,
And his wool so white,
Oh, he is my darling, my heart's delight!"
And the mother-sheep and her little one
Side by side lay down in the sun;
And they went to sleep on the hill-side warm,
While my little lammie lies here on my arm.

I went to the kitchen, and what did I see
But the old gray cat with her kittens three!
I heard her whispering soft: said she,
" My kittens, with tails so cunningly curled,
Are the prettiest things that can be in the world.
The bird on the tree,
And the old ewe she,
May love their babies exceedingly;
But I love my kittens there,
Under the rocking-chair.
I love my kittens with all my might,
I love them at morning, noon, and night.

Now I'll take up my kitties, the kitties I love,
And we'll lie down together beneath the warm
    stove."
Let the kittens sleep under the stove so warm,
While my little darling lies here on my arm.

I went to the yard, and I saw the old hen
Go clucking about with her chickens ten;
She clucked and she scratched and she bustled
    away,
And what do you think I heard the hen say?
I heard her say, " The sun never did shine
On anything like to these chickens of mine.
You may hunt the full moon and the stars, if you
    please,
But you never will find ten such chickens as these.
My dear, downy darlings, my sweet little things,
Come, nestle now cozily under my wings."
So the hen said,
And the chickens all sped
As fast as they could to their nice feather bed.
And there let them sleep, in their feathers so
    warm,
While my little chick lies here on my arm.

                          Mrs. Carter.

How They Sleep

Some things go to sleep in such a funny way:
Little birds stand on one leg and tuck their heads
away;

Chickens do the same, standing on their perch;
Little mice lie soft and still as if they were in
church;

Kittens curl up close in such a funny ball;
Horses hang their sleepy heads and stand still in
a stall;

Sometimes dogs stretch out, or curl up in a heap;
Cows lie down upon their sides when they would
go to sleep.

But little babies dear are snugly tucked in beds,
Warm with blankets, all so soft, and pillows for
their heads.

Bird and beast and babe—I wonder which of all
Dream the dearest dreams that down from
dreamland fall!

Unknown.

Baby-Land

Which is the way to Baby-Land?
    Any one can tell;
        Up one flight,
        To your right;
    Please to ring the bell.

What can you see in Baby-Land?
    Little folks in white,
        Downy heads,
        Cradle-beds,
    Faces pure and bright.

What do they do in Baby-Land?
    Dream and wake and play,
        Laugh and crow,
        Shout and grow,
    Jolly times have they.

What do they say in Baby-Land?
    Why, the oddest things;
        Might as well
        Try to tell
    What a birdie sings.

Who is the queen of Baby-Land?
  Mother kind and sweet;
    And her love,
    Born above,
  Guides the little feet.

George Cooper.

Lullaby

Baby wants a lullaby;
  Where should mother find it?
In a bird's nest rocked on high;
  Birdie, birdie lined it;
Find it under birdie's wing,—
  Soft birdie's feather;—
O the downy, downy thing!
  O the summer weather!

Baby wants a lullaby;
  Where shall sister find it?
In a soft cloud of the sky,
  With white wool behind it;
Watch you may, but cannot guess
  If the cloud has motion,
Such a perfect calm there is
  In the airy ocean.

O the land of Lullabies!
  Where shall father find it?
Safe in mother's breast it lies,
  With her arms to bind it;
O a soft and sleepy song!
  Sleep, baby blossom!
Sleep is short, sleep is long,
  Sweet is mother's bosom!

                    William Brighty Rands.

A Cradle Song

What does little birdie say
In her nest at peep of day?
Let me fly, says little birdie,
Mother, let me fly away.
Birdie, rest a little longer,
Till the little wings are stronger.
So she rests a little longer,
Then she flies away.

What does little baby say,
In her bed at peep of day?
Baby says, like little birdie,
Let me rise and fly away.

Baby, sleep a little longer,
Till the little limbs are stronger.
If she sleeps a little longer,
Baby too shall fly away.

Alfred, Lord Tennyson.

Good-night Prayer for a Little Child

Father, unto Thee I pray,
Thou hast guarded me all day;
Safe I am while in Thy sight,
Safely let me sleep to-night.

Bless my friends, the whole world bless,
Help me to learn helpfulness;
Keep me ever in Thy sight:
So to all I say Good-night.

Henry Johnstone.

The Sleepy Song *

As soon as the fire burns red and low
 And the house upstairs is still,
She sings me a queer little sleepy song,
 Of sheep that go over the hill.

---

* From " Poems," copyright, 1903, by Chas. Scribner's Sons.

The good little sheep run quick and soft,
   Their colors are gray and white;
They follow their leader nose and tail,
   For they must be home by night.

And one slips over, and one comes next,
   And one runs after behind;
The gray one's nose at the white one's tail,
   The top of the hill they find.

And when they get to the top of the hill
   They quietly slip away,
But one runs over and one comes next—
   Their colors are white and gray.

And over they go, and over they go,
   And over the top of the hill
The good little sheep run quick and soft,
   And the house upstairs is still.

And one slips over and one comes next,
   The good little, gray little sheep!
I watch how the fire burns red and low,
   And she says that I fall asleep.

                Josephine Daskam Bacon.

Minnie and Winnie

Minnie and Winnie
  Slept in a shell.
Sleep, little ladies!
  And they slept well.

Pink was the shell within,
  Silver without;
Sounds of the great sea
  Wandered about.

Sleep, little ladies!
  Wake not soon!
Echo on echo
  Dies to the moon.

Two bright stars
  Peeped into the shell.
" What are they dreaming of?
  Who can tell? "

Started a green linnet
  Out of the croft;
Wake, little ladies!
  The sun is aloft.

          Alfred, Lord Tennyson.

Queen Mab

A little fairy comes at night;
　Her eyes are blue, her hair is brown,
With silver spots upon her wings,
　And from the moon she flutters down.

She has a little silver wand,
　And when a good child goes to bed,
She waves her wand from right to left,
　And makes a circle round its head.

And then it dreams of pleasant things—
　Of fountains filled with fairy fish,
And trees that bear delicious fruit,
　And bow their branches at a wish;

Of arbors filled with dainty scents
　From lovely flowers that never fade,
Bright flies that glitter in the sun,
　And glow-worms shining in the shade;

And talking birds with gifted tongues
　For singing songs and telling tales,
And pretty dwarfs to show the way
　Through fairy hills and fairy dales.

　　　　　　　　　　　Thomas Hood.

A Boy's Mother *

My mother she's so good to me,
Ef I was good as I could be,
I couldn't be as good—no, sir!—
Can't any boy be good as her.

She loves me when I'm glad er sad;
She loves me when I'm good er bad;
An', what's a funniest thing, she says
She loves me when she punishes.

I don't like her to punish me,—
That don't hurt,—but it hurts to see
Her cryin'.—Nen *I* cry; an' nen
We both cry an' be good again.

She loves me when she cuts an' sews
My little cloak an' Sund'y clothes;
An' when my Pa comes home to tea,
She loves him most as much as me.

She laughs an' tells him all I said,
An' grabs me up an' pats my head;
An' I hug *her*, an' hug my Pa,
An' love him purt' nigh much as Ma.

James Whitcomb Riley.

* From "*Rhymes of Childhood*," copyright, 1905, and by special permission of the publishers, The Bobbs-Merrill Company.

Our Mother

Hundreds of stars in the pretty sky,
  Hundreds of shells on the shore together,
Hundreds of birds that go singing by,
  Hundreds of birds in the sunny weather,

Hundreds of dewdrops to greet the dawn,
  Hundreds of bees in the purple clover,
Hundreds of butterflies on the lawn,
  But only one mother the wide world over.

                                    Unknown.

Said I to myself, here's a chance for me,
The Lilliput Laureate for to be!
And these are the Specimens I sent in
To Pinafore Palace.   Shall I win?

William Brighty Rands

INDEX

241